RETURN OF THE PESTS

EMER STAMP

HODDER CHILDREN'S BOOKS

First published in Great Britain in 2021
by Hodder & Stoughton

1 3 5 7 9 10 8 6 4 2

A CIP catalogue record for this book
is available from the British Library.

ISBN 978 1 444 94964 3

Printed and bound in Great Britain by Clays Ltd, Elcograf S.p.A.

The paper and board used in this book are made
from wood from responsible sources.

MIX
Paper from
responsible sources
FSC
www.fsc.org **FSC® C104740**

Hodder Children's Books
An imprint of
Hachette Children's Group
Part of Hodder & Stoughton
Carmelite House
50 Victoria Embankment
London EC4Y 0DZ

An Hachette UK Company

www.hachette.co.uk
www.hachettechildrens.co.uk

The PESTS Test (Part 2)

Answer these simple questions
to find out how pesty you are ...

1. You find an old lump of cheesy pasta on the floor. Do you:

A) Brush it up

B) Have it for your dinner

C) Squish it into the floor with your foot

2. You come across a mans sleeping in their bed. Do you:

A) Sing them a lullaby

B) Wake them up by scrabbling and scratching around

C) Tiptoe away

3. You, by mistake, eat a whole packet of biscuits. Do you:

A) Replace the packet

B) Make it look like a dog/cat/grandparent ate them

C) Apologise

4. You find a bag of rubbish left by the bin. Do you:

A) Avoid it, it smells gross

B) Tear it open and spread it all around making an epic mess

C) Put it in the bin

5. You find yourself on a garden trampoline. Do you:

A) Have a bounce

B) Poop on it and run away

C) Do an impressive summersault

Read bottom of page to see what the results mean

If you answered all As and Cs then STOP READING this book immediately. You will never be a PEST. If you answered all Bs, congratulations, read on, you are just the kind of creature P.E.S.T.s. is looking for.

STIX

MEET TH

DR. KRAPOTKIN

BLUE

GRANDMA

E PESTS

MAXIMUS

BATZ

THE PLAGUES

DUG

UNDERLAY

WEBBO

I'M BACK

This is me, Stix, and
I am the height of a
pepper pot — the glass one
that sits in the middle
of the kitchen table next
to the ketchup and the
salt. It's quite a bit
bigger than the egg cup
I was the height of
last time I measured
myself, so I am
very pleased.

Nest

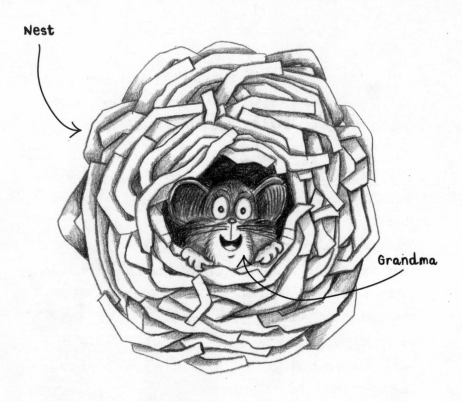

Grandma

I live with my grandma in a nest hidden behind the washing machine of Flat 3, Peewit Mansions. It's the only home I have ever known. Until recently I had never even been out of the flat. But that all changed when I met my best friend, Batz – she's a bat, but I'm guessing that's obvious from the name.

Batz told me all about the school in the basement – a school for pests like me and her. It's called **The Peewit Educatorium for Seriously Terrible Scoundrels**, or **P.E.S.T.S.** for short. At **P.E.S.T.S.** we learn how to be the best pests we can be – how to make the biggest nuisances of ourselves, and have fun bothering the mans – but without getting caught.

I joined at the end of the year, which was tough as I had to catch up, but I'm really glad I did. I learnt loads, though at the end of term stuff did get pretty hairy. This crazy cockroach tried to blow up the whole of Peewit Mansions, with all of us inside it! Batz and I managed to stop him, which was kind of exciting. I can't wait for school to start again tonight, though I hope there won't be another adventure THAT big again.

But first – **it's dinnertime!** Just like always, we wait till the mans we live with have gone to bed and then we sneak out and look for food.

Our mans aren't so bad – they're called Schnookums,

MyLove, Boo-Boo, and they have a dog called **Trevor**.

Boo-Boo

Schnookums

MyLove

Tonight, we're in luck — they had cheesy bake! Besides pizza this is my most favourite food. I guess Boo-Boo doesn't like it that much. I find a huge blob of it on the step of her highchair and another smear on the door of the saucepan cupboard – she must have flicked it really hard to get it that far.

I split the lump on the highchair in two, but Grandma says she isn't hungry. Which is odd – it's not like Grandma to turn down food, especially something as yummy as this.

After eating almost nothing, Grandma goes back to bed.

But I'm not tired. I've still got lots of energy and I want to have some fun.

At this time of night, it's always just me and Trevor, the sausage-shaped dog. Trevor's a funny creature. I don't mean in a Ha-ha! way, I mean in a grumpy one. Until recently he used to get cross that Grandma and I lived in the kitchen and the mans didn't know. Whenever he saw us, he'd bark and bark, trying to tell them, but of course they couldn't understand him. Mans are so stupid – they can't understand any creatures but themselves.

Trevor stopped being quite so cross after I helped him save Boo-Boo from the Plagues, Maximus's pet fleas. (Maximus, by the way, is the big horrible rat who goes to

P.E.S.T.S. and the one creature I am NOT looking forward to seeing.)

Anyway, flea defeating aside, I'm still not sure I can trust Trevor. He's a dog, after all. Grandma has a phrase: **Look a dog in the eye, seconds later you will die.**

Grandma has a lot of phrases like this. Her favourite one is: **A seen mouse is a dead mouse.** She's very strict about how we behave. Not being seen is a really important rule at P.E.S.T.S. too, but we are also taught about having a little fun while the mans aren't looking. Those are the lessons that I love best!

Luckily, Trevor is always asleep when I am awake, so I don't worry too much about him seeing me. Tonight, as usual, he's snoring on his fluffy dog bed next to the fridge. I have this game I like to play with him. Well, when I say 'with', I mean more like I play and he lies there asleep. It's called THE STIX SPECTACULAR. I started off jumping the tip of his tail and over time I've practised and got better and better. I'm working my way up to being able to jump over his bottom. I'm getting really good at it.

I need a long run-up, so I head for the far corner of

the kitchen. I take four deep breaths (my lucky number) and then begin my run. I'm getting faster and faster, but just as I reach my take-off point, Trevor lets out this unbelievably long and noisy fart. I've never heard anything like it! I'm so distracted that I take off all wrong and, rather than somersault over his bottom, I find myself tumbling into his soft, squishy tummy. I bounce off, landing not far from his nose.

Trevor growls and my legs turn to jelly ... I want to run, but spine-tingling fear has me frozen to the spot.

I look up at Trevor and see him staring straight at me. **Looking me straight in the eye ...**

NEW DIET

I do the only thing I can think to do. I hold my paws out in front of me, like somehow they are going to save me.

'MOUSE!' he growls.

'I'm s-sorry ...' I stammer. I peek through my fingers at him. I notice Trevor's expression has shifted from one of anger to confusion.

'WHAT YOU DOING, MOUSE?'

'I was just ... err ... trying to jump over your, umm ... don't hurt me!' I squeak.

'Why I do that?'

'B-because, err ... you're a dog and I, err ... woke you ... though it wasn't my fault! Your huge fart distracted me and I, err, tripped and fell.'

Trevor is silent for a moment. I feel every muscle in my body tense. Can I make it back to the washing machine before he catches me?

Then he lets out a chuckle. 'New diet!' he grins. 'High-protein dried food. Does bad things to Trevor's tummy.'

'Oh ... right,' I say, breathing a sigh of relief. 'Well, umm ... it's late, I'd best be getting off to—'

'Shhh, mouse, Trevor sleeping now,' he huffs, lying his head back on his paws and closing his eyes. His tummy lets out a dangerous-sounding grumble.

The second his eyes are closed, I dash back to our nest, furious with myself for so nearly getting into trouble. I really should obey Grandma's rules. And I usually do. Like, 99 per cent of the time.

OK, maybe more like 95.6 per cent.

When you're a young mouse, you can't obey ALL the rules – if you did, you'd have no fun.

P.E.S.T.S.
HERE I COME

I fall asleep thinking about Batz and all the fun we are going to have at school. I'm just in the middle of a dream where I discover I can fly too, when I'm woken by a worrying noise. It sounds like someone or something is eating our nest. I sit up, rubbing furiously at my bleary eyes.

Where's Grandma? What's going on?

"Orry,' I hear her say. I turn and there she is, sitting next to me, mouth stuffed

10

with paper. 'I 'idn't 'ean to 'ake 'ou.' She swallows hard and smiles.

'Is that a ... letter?' I say, noticing the scribble of mans words on the final shred she's shoving into her mouth.

'Yes,' she declares, finishing up. 'I had a sudden craving for biro ink. And that totally hit the spot.'

My grandma is so strange! I guess this isn't THAT unusual. She often does weird things, like:

- **tying knots in her tail to remember things**
- **eating food so spicy it makes her hiccup**
- **clicking her fingers and toes all at once** (just because she can).

Eating letters does seem VERY odd though, even by Grandma's standards. But I guess it's just another one to add to the list.

'Come on, my boy, let's get back to sleep,' she says, snuggling down and wrapping herself around me. 'We want you on top form for the first night of school now, don't we?'

When I wake hours later she's still asleep, so I creep out into the kitchen alone. It's dark and, apart from the whirr of the fridge, completely silent. The clock on the cooker says 11.08. Still nearly an hour before school starts.

I waste 34 minutes finding food. After a lot of searching I finally find two very old, very dried chips behind the bin and a large glob of cereal welded to the bottom of Boo-Boo's chair. I scrape it off and divide it in two, leaving half for Grandma.

I decide to kill the rest of the time practising one of my new Stix Skills — these are special moves I invent, I'm adding to them all the time. This evening I'm going to practise THE STIX SQUEEZE. Basically, I have to fit myself into the smallest space I can find.

I start off with the toe of MyLove's slipper. It's rather smelly, but very easy.

A slightly harder test is one of Boo-Boo's much smaller shoes. I still manage it.

I look around for something even trickier ... The little finger of the left washing-up glove. It's a tight squeeze ... but — yes! — I manage it.

For my finale I choose one of Boo-Boo's toy cars I find discarded in the hallway. I'm just wrestling the final part of myself in, when I hear Grandma.

'Evening, darling,' she says, peering in through the small car's tiny windscreen. **'What are you doing in there? Isn't it time for school?'**

I scramble out of the car and glance up at the clock. 11.55. How have I gone from being way too early for school to being seriously late?!

I give Grandma a quick goodbye hug and scamper up the kitchen drawers. Quick as I can, I slide down into the kitchen sink and skid over to the plughole. This is the entrance to the hidden highway for Flat 3, the secret tunnel that takes you all the way down to P.E.S.T.S. in the basement.

I wiggle myself down through the plughole and into the waste pipe below.

I let go, and feel my body start to slide.

Wooooo-hoooooo! P.E.S.T.S. here I come!

PROFESSOR DUG

In no time at all I reach the basement. I tumble out of the tunnel and my nose fills with the familiar smell of old paper, stale clothes and dusty furniture.

I've been trained well enough by Grandma to know that no matter how familiar you are with somewhere, you never run straight out. I place my nose on CSM **(Constant Sniff Mode)** and tiptoe, using a new silent-stepping technique I've been working on, through the piles of boxes and stacks of old junk, towards the tatty old wardrobe that is our classroom.

Tiptoe, sniff, sniff, tiptoe.

My heart starts beating faster, the fur along my back stands on end and my paws begin to tingle. My inbuilt 'mouse fear' seems to have kicked in. We mice are naturally always so careful, always so cautiou—

SWOOSH!

BOOMPH!

Something hits me, sending me tumbling across the floor into an old roll of carpet. I let out an involuntary squeak of terror as a cloud of dust erupts around me.

'Heehahahahaha. Didn't see that coming, did ya?' laughs a familiar voice.

'BATZ!' I choke crossly. 'You scared me! I thought ... I thought I was being attacked!'

'Well, you were ... by me! Heehahahaha!' She laughs and laughs, pressing her big bat face up close to mine and crossing her eyes. 'Good to see you for real, in the flesh,' she says, pulling back. 'By the way, have you grown? You look taller. I mean not that much, a fraction, a titchy bit, I'd say a smidge, a lit—'

'Good to see you too, Batz,' I interrupt. I'd forgotten just how much my best friend likes to talk. I can't stay angry with her though. There is something about her that makes it impossible. I can't help but smile.

'It's been ages,' I say.

'I know, too long. Come on, let's go — if we don't hurry up, we're going to be late.' And a moment later she's flying off towards the wardrobe. 'Stix and Batz,' she sings, 'Batz and Stix. Together again. Dum-dee-doo.' It's terribly out of tune, which just makes me laugh more.

We reach the tatty old lamp that lies propped up

against the wardrobe, the route up to the classroom for those of us who can't fly. In my excitement, I scurry up so quickly that as I reach the top, I lose my footing and trip off the end. I tumble across the floor of the wardrobe, coming to a halt at a pair of broad pink feet.

'Well, hello, Stix. Good to see you!' says Dug the mole with a smile, offering me a large paw.

'Dude!' cries Webbo the spider, galloping over. 'Give me seven,' he says, hi-fiving me while balancing on one leg.

'Hellostixmyoldfriendthoughyouarenotactuallythatoldso morelikeayoungfriendreally,' gabbles Underlay the carpet beetle, poking her head out from around Dug's large tummy. I manage to catch the words 'hello' and 'friend'.

Blue takes great pleasure in buzzing his large bluebottle body around my head super

fast. My eyes try and keep up, but I soon become dizzy and have to stop.

Above me, Batz settles herself on the clothes rail.

'It's so great to see you all,' I say, unable to stop my face breaking into a stupidly big grin.

'And it's great to see you, too ... mini mouse,' I hear a horribly familiar voice snigger from behind me. A bitter scent hits my nose and my heart sinks. I spin round just in time to see a large rat leap off the end of the lamp and on to the wardrobe floor. He lands with a heavy thump. It's **Maximus**, the class bully, who last term made it his mission to ruin my life. I'd hoped after all the trouble he got himself into at the end of the year, he would be a bit nicer – clearly not.

He shakes his body and pulls himself up to his full height. He's gone from giant to **gigantic**, and now looks even more capable of doing horrible things to me. I fight the urge to run to the back of the wardrobe and hide.

'Woah, someone had a maHOOssive growth spurt!' Webbo says with a grin.

'Yeah, I have. So you all better watch it!' snarls

Maximus. I can't believe it – even his teeth are bigger. He pushes his way to the back of the classroom, while rubbing his left ear with his paw.

'What happened to your ear? You got growing pains in it?' asks Webbo, still chuckling away.

Maximus pulls his paw away. I notice that his ear looks red and sore.

'I hurt it fighting a cat,' he mutters. 'The cat came off a lot **worse**.'

'A cat? Really?' I hear a high-pitched voice come from somewhere on his body, followed by another: 'You couldn't beat up a cat-ERPILLAR.'

It's the fleas that live in his fur, Plague One and Plague

Two. They're sitting on his shoulder, falling about laughing like they've just made the funniest joke ever.

'**Be quiet!**' Maximus growls, slapping at them. He plonks himself down directly behind me. I stare straight ahead, determined not to

show how scared I am of him. The rest of the class has gone quiet too.

And that's when I realise something's wrong. Our teacher, Dr Krapotkin — a hell-raising pigeon with a big ringed 'A' for Anarchy emblazoned on her chest — isn't here yet. She always gets to class before us. Tonight, all that's at the front of the class is a rusty old tin of red paint.

'Where izzzzzz she?' buzzes Blue.

'Maybeshe'sforgottenschoolstartstonight,' gabbles Underlay.

'Ace! An extra day of holiday!' cheers Webbo, clapping his legs.

'Probably just a bit late, that's all,' says Dug so quietly even I have to strain my ears to hear him. 'Maybe we should just get on and start without her? I could suggest something we could do, if you like?'

'The mole wants to play teacher,' Maximus laughs cruelly. 'Ha! Ha! I'd like to see the whispering wally try.'

'At least he's got the brains to do it. Who was Pest of the Year last year?' says Batz. She points her wing at Dug. 'Him, not you.'

Maximus shoots her a look of disgust and in return Batz pokes out her tongue. She's so funny, I love her so much.

'I think Dug will make a great stand-in teacher,' I say, patting him on his large furry shoulder. 'What do you think we should do, Dug?'

'Well,' he says, raising his voice a fraction louder, 'I was thinking we could start with a show and tell ... you know, demonstrate something we have learnt over the break.'

'Goodideateacherdug,' says Underlay, giving him a big thumbs up. 'Iwillgofirstifyoulike? Checkthisoutforfast!' She jumps out of the wardrobe and, in a matter of seconds, she chews the old rug in the centre of the basement in two. 'Beenpractisingafasterchomp,' she declares proudly.

Next up, Webbo shows off his new 'super-hairy legs', which apparently have grown twice as long over the holiday. He proudly demonstrates their superior tickling power on Dug, who is soon in fits of giggles, wriggling on the floor,

begging for him to stop.

　　Next up, Blue shows us his new 'rocket zzzpeed'. He circles our heads so fast that we can't even see him.

　　Then Batz shows us this hilarious thing she calls the **'Ghost Bat'**. She flits over to a big bag of something or other, tucked away on a wobbly old set of shelves on the other side of the basement, and disappears inside it. Seconds later she bursts out again, but this time she's a ghostly shade of white.

'Woah!' says Webbo. 'Spooky! What is that?'

'Cement powder,' she says, grinning. 'I've only tried it with flour before, but this works just as well.' She then proceeds to swoop over us, making eerie squeaking noises and dousing us all with a thin layer of powder.

Dug announces that he has been teaching himself to write mans, which he says is not necessarily a mole talent, but one he is clearly very proud of. Using a long claw he scratches the letters 'HELO' into the floor of the wardrobe.

We all clap, apart from Maximus, who yawns loudly. 'Is that really all you've got?' he says, his words clearly wounding poor Dug. 'Well, the best should be saved for last, and since there's two of us left, looks like it's your turn, loser.' He shoves me forward.

I ignore him and make my way over to the side of the wardrobe. I've decided to show off my Paw Stand – another new skill I've been working on. If nothing else, I hope it will impress Batz. I place my paws on the ground and flick my back legs up. I look up at Batz

and smile. Now we are both upside down – which makes her the right way up for once!

'Awesome!' she cries, waving excitedly at me.

I lower my feet back down, feeling pretty pleased with myself.

Maximus rolls his eyes. 'OK, losers, now it's time for ME to show you what REAL skill is. Because I've been learning how to chew through LIVE electrical cables,' he boasts. 'If I can just find one, I'll show you numpties how it's done ...'

'Err, I don't think so, darlink,' says a voice from the other side of the basement. It's Dr Krapotkin at last. With a soft flap of her wings she swoops across the room, skimming over Maximus's head and landing neatly on her one good foot, on top of the paint tin.

'No chomping cables on my watch. I can't have one of my pupils making a mistake and blowing themselves up now, can I?'

We all let out a small gasp, but it's not her words that have shocked us. It's her appearance. She looks terrible. Her feathers are wild and messy and both her small and large eyes have a wild look in them – even wilder than usual –

like she hasn't slept for a long time.

'Well, don't just sit there staring,' she says, taking up her usual position at the front of the wardrobe. 'Switch your brains on, it's time for class.'

'Woah,' whispers a worried-sounding Dug. 'That's one super-stressed-looking pigeon.'

DR KRAP—
WHAT?—KIN

'So, good evening, darlinks,' says Dr Krapotkin briskly,
brushing down her untidy feathers. I notice she no longer
has the large anarchic 'A' painted across her chest. 'Many
apologies for my tardiness. Good to see you have been
keeping yourselves amused in my absence.' She glances down
at the floor next to Dug's feet. 'For the record, there are
two Ls in "Hello". But this is a wonderful new skill, Dug!
Very impressive, darlink. Now, to start the new term I
would like to introduce you to the new, revised rules of
P.E.S.T.S.'

'New rules?' whispers Dug, sounding surprised.

Dr Krapotkin pulls a lump of chalk from under a tatty wing and, on the blackboard, in large capital letters, writes:

1. A GOOD PEST IS NEVER SEEN

GOOD PEST IS NEVER SEEN

3. A GOOD PEST IS NEVER SEEN

4. A GOOD PEST IS NEVER SEEN

5. A GOOD PEST IS NEVER SEEN

She's clearly made a mistake; perhaps her brain is as jumbled as her feathers. Where are the old rules? A good pest is heard but never seen; a good pest is always one step ahead; a good pest bothers but never harms; a good pest has fun but covers its tracks; a good pest never goes too far.

'Err, but they're all the same?' says Webbo.

'Indeed they are. That is because this is the only rule that is important now. Our sole focus this term is to keep ourselves safe and hidden. There will be no pestiness, no bothering, no messing around; there will be no having of the fun. Do you get me, darlinks?'

My heart sinks. I've been so looking forward to coming back to school and doing lots of exciting stuff. Surely she must be joking.

'And that ...' she says, pausing as if momentarily lost in thought, '... will be all for this evening. You are free to leave. Just remember rules one, two, three, four and five.'

I glance up at Batz. She looks as surprised as me. This is strange even by Dr Krapotkin's odd standards.

'Chippidy-chop, darlinks,' she says, herding us out with

her large wings. 'Off you go.'

'Woah, I mean, what was that all about?' says Batz, as we make our way back across the basement. 'It's like they took out her anarchic brain and put in a super-boring one instead.'

'Can someone really do that?' I reply, horrified at the thought.

'No, silly, of course they can't.' She laughs, swooping down and giving me a playful shoulder nudge. 'I'm just messing with you. **But something odd's going on, that's for sure.**'

'Yeah,' I say. 'Let's hope whatever's happened to her unhappens fast.'

'Couldn't agree more, amigo,' she chortles. 'Well, see you tomorrow, I guess.' And with a shrug she flits off and out through the air vent at the top of the wall.

As I head for the hidden highway back to Flat 3, I feel very disappointed that tonight wasn't quite the fun first day back I'd hoped for.

NOT AGAIN, GRANDMA!

I get back to our nest just before dawn. School might not have been very exciting, but I'm still pooped. However, it hardly feels I've been asleep at all when I'm woken by the sound of munching, again. I can't believe it – **Grandma's eating another letter!** I left her a perfectly good-sized blob of cereal for dinner – why would she need to eat a letter as well?

She finishes and lets out a small burp that smells strongly of biro ink.

'Are you ... OK?' I ask.

'Oh, yes, dear boy, I'm just fine,' she replies chirpily. 'Your old grandma is just tickety-boo. All the better for having eaten that. Biro ink, yum!'

As I drift off back to sleep I can't help feeling that she's not telling me the truth. But I don't know what else to say or ask. I think about the first day at school and how odd Dr Krapotkin was. **Why are both the elders in my life behaving so strangely?**

I wake feeling more tired than when I went to bed. Grandma is still asleep as I make my way out into the kitchen.

From the boxes by the door, I know it's been pizza night. This cheers me a little. The mans always leave a few crusts in the box, and these days sometimes even a slice. Grandma says Schnookums is on something the mans call a 'diet' which is a very strange thing indeed. Who wouldn't want to eat ALL their food? Not me, for sure! Especially not when it's pizza. I LOVE pizza. With all that yummy cheese, what mouse wouldn't?

My mouth starts watering before I've even reached the

boxes. I wiggle inside and am just wrestling a long, chewy line of delicious mozzarella into my mouth when I hear the faint sound of an unfamiliar mans coming from The Beyond — the area on the other side of The Frontier Door. Whoever it is, is in the hallway outside the flat. The only other mans I ever hear is Tarquin from Flat 4. But it's not him. And there aren't often visitors on this floor; not this late at night, anyway.

I clamber out of the pizza box and press my ear to the door. The mans is talking to someone. But I can't make out what he's saying.

I am **expressly forbidden** from going out into The Beyond — another of Grandma's many rules — but I'm DYING to see who it is. Who would be walking along our corridor so late at night?

I'll just slide under the door and have a little peek and then slide back. Grandma will never have to know. I mean, honestly, what harm can it do?

STRANGER DANGER

I press myself flat to the floor and wiggle my body underneath the door. I squeeze out the other side, then flatten myself against the doorframe.

In front of the large window at the end of the hallway, silhouetted in the moonlight, I see the shape of a mans. His sweet, sickly scent hits my nose, making me want to gag.

The only thing I can really make out about him is his bizarre hair. It sits on top of his head like a crashing wave of water.

As he moves, I catch a glimpse of something else: some

kind of creature
tucked into the
crook of his arm.
It looks like a cross
between a dog
and a mop.

In the other
hand the mans is
holding a spray
can, the same
size and shape as
the one MyLove
uses to clean the
furniture. But
something tells me
this mans is not
here to polish.

'Mummy may
have turned a
blind eye to you,
my hairy-legged

little friend, but sadly for you she's gone now.' The mans leans forward to address a tiny black dot on the wall. 'So, I'm in charge. And you know what that means?' His voice suddenly switches from soft and caring to harsh and cruel. **'It means your time is up.** But don't be too sad. Yes, you are going to die, horribly and painfully, but you will also have the privilege of being the first to be sprayed with my new improved KILLING formula. Isn't he such a lucky boy, Duchy-poo?'

The mop-dog lets out a sharp yap and the black dot suddenly shoots up the wall. Quick as a flash, the mans hoses it in spray and the dot stops dead in its tracks and falls to the floor.

'Don't worry, death will come swiftly,' cackles the mans, turning and walking back down the corridor, straight towards me. I tuck myself even tighter into the doorframe, praying he won't see me as he strides down the corridor in his big black shoes, which I notice are pointed and very shiny. I hold my breath as he gets closer and closer ... so close I can smell his shoe polish ... then he walks on past me.

I let out a sigh of relief as he reaches the other end of the hallway. But then he does something very unexpected. He goes up the stairs, rather than down. Why would he do that? Grandma says there is only something called 'the attic', up there, which is just the storage space at the top of the block. No one lives there.

But I don't have time to give it any further thought

because, from the other end of the hallway, I hear a faint, croaky cry. The poor creature the mans sprayed! I rush over and find an old spider. His body is shuddering and his long legs are curled up tightly around him.

'Urgh! He got me good 'n' proper!' he rasps. 'This hallway used to be a safe haven ... not any more! Cruel, nasty mans. Killing me, and all for what? A nice clean wall? He doesn't care I got a wife and three hundred and twenty-two children to look after. You need to get away from here, mouse,' he says, prising a weak leg from his body and trying to shoo me away. 'Before he gets you as well. That's what he does, **him** – he's a pest-killing machine!'

The poor spider's body judders violently and all four of his eyes roll in his head.

'But I can't just leave you here, like this!' I protest.

'The toxins are at work already. A young 'un like you's got no chance of savin' me.'

'Then I'll take you to an elder,' I say, and before I've even had the chance to think through what I am suggesting, I pull him up on to my back and start running as

quickly as I can down the hallway.

It's nearly time for P.E.S.T.S.; if I can just get him to Dr Krapotkin, I'm sure she'll be able to help.

As I pass by the door of Flat 4, I notice it's ajar. I catch a glimpse inside. All Tarquin's stuff is gone — replaced by some strange-looking machines. But I've no time to wonder about that either. I have a dying spider on my back and I need to get him to the basement. **FAST!**

SPIDER CPR

By the time I reach the basement, the spider is unconscious. **'Quick, he needs help!'** I shout. I carry him the final few steps up the lampshade, then lie him gently on the floor of the wardrobe.

'UNCLE MELVIN! What's going on? What's happened to him?' cries Webbo, rushing forwards.

Before I can answer, Dr Krapotkin bends over his lifeless body and takes a deep sniff. The rest of the class gather around her, trying to get a look. 'Acephate,' she declares. 'With trace elements of bendiocarb. A very powerful and deadly concoction. His body is shutting down. Where did you find him, darlink?'

'In the hallway,' I pant, trying to catch my breath. 'Outside my flat. He got sprayed.'

'OK, everyone, I need you to stand well back. I'm going to perform CPR — that's cardiopulmonary resuscitation, darlinks ... in case you didn't know. Watch and learn — you never know when you might need to do this yourselves.'

She reaches down and gently draws the spider's mouth open,

then carefully pokes the very tip of her beak in and blows. The spider's chest immediately rises. She watches it fall and then does the same again. On the third breath, the spider's body suddenly jolts back to life and he is sick all over the floor.

'Excellent!' she declares, sidestepping the green slime. 'The body is repelling the toxins. Once they are all out, you'll feel much more like your spider-self again, darlink.'

The spider looks up at her and nods, then vomits again.

'**Oh my, that really is a very unnatural colour,**' winces Dug, shuffling backwards.

Remarkably, after just a few minutes, Webbo's uncle is back on his feet – albeit a little shakily. Webbo rushes over, and they hug in a weird, many-legged embrace.

'Did you get eyes on the perpetrator, darlink?' asks Dr

Krapotkin. 'Did you see the cruel mans who did this to you?'

'Indeed, I did,' says the spider, gravely. 'It was **HIM**.'

Dr Krapotkin shudders. 'I knew it,' she mutters under her breath. 'I knew we couldn't contain him. Darlinks, I must leave immediately; there is a dear friend I need to consult without a moment's delay. Good night to you all.'

And with that she flies off, leaving us all rather perplexed.

'Woah, this just gets weirder and weirder,' says Batz, gliding along next to me as I make my way across the basement towards the hidden highway. 'Top job on saving Uncle Melvin, though!'

'Thanks,' I say shyly. 'I'm sure anyone would have done the same.'

'Take a compliment!' She laughs, punching my shoulder with her wing. **'You're a hero!'**

'Hey, fancy a game of hide and seek?' I suggest eagerly.

'Err, yeah, about that ... I'd love to but ...' she says, shifting around awkwardly, '... I can't, not right now

... gotta see a bat about a gnat. Catch you tomorrow, though!'

And, just like that, she swoops off.

What was all that about? Why is she in such a hurry to get away? We haven't had a chance to play in for ever.

No sooner has she disappeared through the small air vent at the top of the wall than I feel a heavy paw on my shoulder and a bitter smell tickles my nostrils. **My stomach lurches - I know immediately who it is.**

'Maximus,' I say as bravely as I can muster, turning around to face him.

'Poor Stix.' He grins. 'Does the bat not want to play with you any more? Has she finally twigged what a loser you are? That's what I've heard. That she wants to dump you and find someone better to be best friends with.'

His words stab at my heart like tiny knives. Surely they can't be true. How could he know anything? He lives in the sewers and she lives in the roof.

'I mean ...' He jabs me with a long-clawed finger. '... I don't blame her. Where's the fun in playing with a boring little mouse?'

'Shut up!' I growl. 'She just had to be somewhere!' He has to be wrong, he must be.

'Did you just answer me back?' he snarls, his paw shooting forward and grabbing my left ear. 'Did you just tell me to shut up?' My ear begins to burn as he cruelly twists it further than I ever thought possible.

'Ow!' I say. 'Please ... stop ...'

But instead he just twists it further. A sharp jolt of pain shoots down my left side.

'Twist it! Twist it!' chant the Plagues, egging him on.

'Nobody,' he says, through clenched teeth, pushing his face into mine, 'nobody EVER answers me back. Do you hear me?'

I want to say, 'No, I can't hear you, because you've got your fat paw wrapped around my ear.' But I figure that would be answering back too. He turns my ear so far, it feels like he might actually twist it off. 'Yes, yes ... I hear you,' I manage to squeak.

He lets go of me and I fall to the floor in a heap, clutching my throbbing ear. My body temperature suddenly soars, I feel like I'm on fire. I never knew it was possible to feel so much anger.

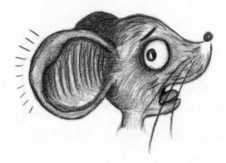

'Loser.' He laughs, booting me with a large foot as he walks away.

I hate him so, SO much. As I make my way back over to the hidden highway, I find myself wishing something terrible, something awful, would happen to him so I never have to see him again.

COLIN ROY-ALE

By the time I reach the kitchen my ear has swollen up to twice its normal size. What am I going to tell Grandma? I run through a list of excuses as I scamper back to our nest. There is no way I am going to tell her the truth. I don't want her coming to P.E.S.T.S. and making a fuss or, worse still, stopping me from going.

But when I get back she's not there. Grandma is ALWAYS in bed at this time. I go back out and do a quick scout of the kitchen, but she's not there either. Maybe she's gone looking for more letters? I really hope not.

I go back to bed and curl up, being careful not to rest my head on my swollen ear. I try not to think about the horrible mans in the attic, or worry about where Grandma is. I tell myself she's too sensible to do anything dangerous or silly, and that I'm sure she'll be back soon, and try to get some sleep.

I must drift off because the next thing I know I'm being woken. But this time it's not Grandma – it's a smell. **A smell that sends ice-cold chills down my spine.**

The smell of the spider sprayer.

I sit up with a start and sniff again. He's close. I prick up my ears and I hear him too. He's talking to MyLove. He's inside the flat!

Quick as a flash, I'm out of the nest and scrabbling up the side of the washing machine and into the basket of washing that is always sitting on it. I clamber to the top of the pile of clean clothes and carefully balance myself on the dome of one of Schnookum's strange, frilly 'bra' things, giving myself a perfect view over the kitchen. It's light – morning, I'm guessing, from the fact Boo-Boo's is sitting in her highchair eating her breakfast.

I know this is dangerous
– mice should never go out in
daylight – but I have to see HIM
and find out why he is here. My
heart starts beating so fast
that I worry it might explode.

'Come in, come in,' says
MyLove, guiding him through into
the kitchen.

Last night all I could see
was his hair and his shiny
shoes, but now I can see all of
him and what an odd-looking
mans he is. His face has a
plastic texture that reminds
me of Boo-Boo's dolls and it's
an unnaturally bright shade of
orange. He wears a suit so white
it positively glows. As he walks
into the kitchen, he brushes at
the sleeve of it – like the flat .

has made him instantly dirty. I press myself into the bra, deciding it's safer to peer out through the basket's slats than over the top.

Under one arm the mans is carrying the mop-dog, which now has a large pink bow tied around a tuft of hair between her ears.

'Hi, I'm Colin, Colin Royale,' he says, holding out an orange hand for MyLove to shake. He pronounces the word 'Royale' like it's two: Roy-Al. His voice is as sweet and sickly as the perfume he's wearing. 'Doris' Peewit's son ... Had to ditch the surname ... seriously, what nit-wit would want to be called Peewit?' He grins, flashing a dazzling set of perfectly straight, very white teeth.

'Ahh, dear Doris, yes, what a love she was. So, so sad to hear that she passed away. Please accept our sincere condolences,' says MyLove.

'And what a wonderful landlord too. So generous,' adds Schnookums.

'Indeed, she was,' smiles Colin, a little too sweetly.

The mop lets out a sharp yelp.

'A dog!' woofs Trevor, waking suddenly from his slumber.

He leaps excitedly from his bed and bounds over.

'Oh, and how could I forget? This little cutie-pie is the Duchess.' Colin smiles, patting her head. 'She's pedigree Pekingese.'

'Hello, friend!' says Trevor, eagerly circling Colin's legs. 'Hello! Hello!'

'Well, this is our Trevor,' smiles MyLove fondly, 'almost, but not quite, pedigree dachshund.'

'Back off, you bone-chomping mongrel. I don't want to catch fleas,' yaps the Duchess, wiggling herself further up Colin's body.

Trevor stops dead in his tracks, clearly thrown by her unfriendly response.

'Err, Trevor no have

fleas. Trevor have flea collar!' he says indignantly.

'Flea collars are for peasants. Dogs with class wear diamonds,' she proclaims, flashing him a glimpse of her glittery collar.

'Aw, how cute. They're having a doggy chat!' says Schnookums, as Trevor slouches back to his bed looking crestfallen. Poor old Trevor.

Colin lets out a small snort. 'I've come for a little chat myself,' he says. 'May I sit?'

'Of course, of course,' says Schnookums, ushering him to the chair next to Boo-Boo's highchair. Colin squeamishly brushes some crumbs of breadstick off the chair and sits, positioning himself on the edge of the seat, as far from the cereal-covered Boo-Boo as he can get.

'Hewow!' she says, waving a milky hand at him.

Colin grimaces back.

'It's all right, she won't bite,' laughs MyLove.

'Yes, me do!' says Boo-Boo, shoving a huge slab of Weetabix into her mouth and chomping it in half. A glob of it dribbles down her chin.

Colin shuffles even further from her and almost falls off the chair. 'Now, I have to say, this is a little awkward,' he says. 'It concerns the matter of the letters I sent you — the ones you appear to have been ignoring?'

'What letters?' says Schnookums, looking very confused.

'We haven't received any letters, have we?' asks MyLove, looking over at Schnookums, who shakes her head and shrugs.

'How very strange,' says Colin, looking between them suspiciously. 'I've been posting them under your door, early every morning, on my way to the gym.' He runs a hand through his hair-wave, pushing it even higher.

Uh-oh, I think. **Is that what Grandma has been eating?**

'Well, I don't have time to dwell on what did or didn't become of them,' he continues curtly. 'I'm here now, so we can discuss the matter face to face.'

'Face!' laughs Boo-Boo, pulling a very funny one. She blows a large raspberry, spraying small bits of Weetabix all around her.

Colin tries to

smile as he squeamishly flicks a blob of milky goo from his brilliant white trousers. 'Now, as you yourselves said, Mummy was exceptionally kind,' he says, turning away from Boo-Boo. 'Some may even say stupidly generous, with the rent she charged.'

'Well ... err ... I ...' splutters Schnookums, suddenly looking rather worried.

'There's no denying it, the dotty old bag ... I mean,' – Colin swiftly corrects himself – 'dear lovely Mama, charged you peanuts.'

'I w-wouldn't go that far,' stammers MyLove, sharing an anxious look with Schnookums.

'Well, I would,' says Colin briskly. 'And, as Mummy left Peewit Mansions to me, I am your new landlord, so it's my opinion that matters. And as your new landlord, I have decided to review the rent.'

'You have?' says MyLove nervously.

'Indeed. The rent for this flat will now be £3,000 a month,' Colin says with a flourish.

'**W... what?**' blusters MyLove, his eyebrows nearly shooting off the top of his head. 'That's over three times what we pay now! We can't afford that.'

'Surely there's room for negotiation,' says Schnookums.

'Nope, there is no room whatsoever,' says Colin coldly. 'That's the price, take it or leave it. Now, if we consult your tenancy agreement ...' he continues, pretending to pull a sheet of paper out of his pocket, '... oh, wait ... you don't have one?' He laughs, waving his empty hand in the air. 'It seems your agreement lapsed some years ago and Mummy never got around to issuing another ... what a shame. Well, don't worry, I'm nothing if not generous. If you haven't got the money, I'll give you a full forty-eight hours to find somewhere else to live.'

Both MyLove's and Schnookum's mouths fall open. 'W-w-what?' stammers MyLove. 'Two DAYS? To find somewhere to live? But that's monstrous ...'

But Colin isn't listening. He rises swiftly to his feet, gathering up the Duchess in his arms.

'I've got WonderScrub booked to do a deep, deep clean the day after tomorrow, so please get all this' – he waves his hand around the room making a face like he's pointing at a disgusting heap of smelly poo – 'cleared out by then. And don't worry. I'll see myself to the door.'

'B-but this isn't fair. You're forcing us out!' splutters Schnookums angrily after him.

'Who said life was fair?' Colin shoots back over his shoulder as he walks out of the door, pulling it closed behind him.

'What are we going to do?' says MyLove.

'We don't have any option but to leave,' says Schnookums, her voice flat. 'I'll call my parents. Hopefully they can have us for a bit while we look for a new flat.'

'Nu fat?' says Boo-Boo, slamming down her spoon. 'Me

no want nu fat. Me wov dis fat.'

'So do we, sweetie,' says MyLove, reaching out and tenderly touching her hand. And as I watch the tears brimming in his eyes, I realise I'm crying too.

A RIGHT ROY-AL MESS

I wipe away my tears with the back of my paw as I scramble back to our nest. My heart feels as heavy as a saucepan as I slump down on to its papery floor. First Colin almost kills Webbo's uncle, and now he's getting rid of the mans too? I know Schnookums and MyLove would probably call Nuke-A-Pest – the nasty company that mans phone when they want to get rid of pests like me - in a heartbeat if they knew we were here, but even so, I've strangely grown fond of them. They're not too clean or tidy so they make it easy for me and Grandma to find food. And I especially like Boo-Boo – she's so funny. And Trevor may be unbelievably grumpy, but he's all right, really.

And what does all this mean for us? I shudder at the thought of a deep, deep clean.

Grandma pointed out an advert for WonderScrub in a newspaper we were tearing up for bedding the other night. It said something like, WonderScrub, the Super-Duper New Cleaning Company from Nuke-A-Pest. One call and we'll bleach it all.

We made a point of tearing the advert into teeny-tiny pieces.

'Oh, Grandma,' I mumble to myself, 'where are you when I need you most?'

'Right here, my boy.'

I spin round and there she is, standing right behind me. I didn't realise old mice could be so sneaky.

'Grandma! I'm so pleased you're back.' I leap up and throw my arms around her. 'A horrible mans, Colin he's called, came and he's making Schnookums, MyLove and Boo-Boo move out. And he's got this nasty dog too and he tried to kill Webbo's uncle and–'

'I know, I know,' she says, clutching me tightly. 'We elders have known about this for a while.'

'You have?' I say, pulling back from her. 'So THAT's why Dr Krapotkin has been behaving so strangely.'

'Yes, we've both been trying to figure out what to do – all the elders are. It's a terrible mess I'm afraid, and the time has come to tell you all about it.' She sits down, wrapping her arm around me, just the way she used to when she told me bedtime stories. 'First you need to know about Doris who, until recently, lived in Flat 5.'

'But aren't there only four flats in the block?' I ask, already confused.

'Kind of yes, kind of no,' replies Grandma. 'Technically,

there are five. It's just that we pests only visit four of them. Doris's flat is — well, I guess I should now say **was** - out of bounds. You see, she was the landlord of the whole place. It was her grandfather that built the building. Doris was a kind and generous mans who was not too fussed about her tenants' levels of cleanliness. Which, of course, suited us pests right down to the ground. More places for us to hide, more food for us to find. So it was decided by the elders, many moons ago — before even I was born — that as a reward we would leave her alone. If we bothered her then there was every chance that she may change her mind and want to tidy things up. So we left her be, all promising never to go near her flat.'

'But now she is gone and Colin has become the landlord?'

'Yes, though what he is doing is NOT what she intended at all. She would never have wanted him to kick out the tenants. They were her friends, she knew them all,' Grandma says despairingly. '**Colin tricked her,** promising her to keep it just the way she did. That's why, when she died, she gladly left it to him. She couldn't see that he was lying — that he just wanted to get his hands on it

65

so he could turf everyone out and turn it into a block of expensive luxury flats. That's what he must be planning.

'He's the worst kind of mans, Stix, the worst of the worst. Not only is he greedy and deceitful, he's also a ... **CLEAN FREAK.**' Grandma practically spits the words. 'He's going to turn our lovely home into a desolate wasteland of cleanliness — a hygienic hellhole. There will be no place left for us.'

'But, can't we do something to stop him? I mean, the elders aren't just going to let him do this, are they? You and Dr Krapotkin have a plan, right?'

'Believe me, we've been trying,' says Grandma, shaking her head sadly. 'We had hoped that if I ate his letters we might stop him getting his mitts on Flat 3, which at least would give us one pest-friendly haven in the block. But now he's come to visit and that's the end of that.'

'Can't we drive him out? Pest him out?' I can't believe what I'm hearing. There must be SOMETHING we can do.

'Colin's a breed apart. He's a one-mans-pest-killing machine. It's a battle too big for us small creatures to fight. And now he's got rid of all the tenants, we have no choice but to leave as well. It's that or be eradicated. He won't stop until he's wiped us all out.'

'B-but this is our home ...' I stammer. 'And what about school? Will I have to leave that too? Leave all my friends?' My heart lurches at the thought of not seeing Batz again.

Grandma places her paws softly on my shoulders, and I immediately know I am not going to like her answer. 'Don't you worry,' she says, with a sad smile. 'You're young. You'll adapt. We'll find a new home. You'll make new friends.'

'But I like the friends I have now!' I shout back at her. 'I don't want to make any new ones. Please, Grandma, surely there's something we can do? There must be!' I beg.

'That's enough now,' she says firmly, removing her paws. 'We can't stay. You heard what Colin said – a deep, deep clean. No mouse can survive that. There will be a final meeting of the elders tonight to agree our exit plan. Now, let's get some sleep. We'll be needing ALL our wits about us from now on.'

'B-b-but ...' I stammer, frantically trying to think of something to say that will keep the conversation going. She has to listen to me? Surely there is something we can do. But Grandma is not listening. She has curled herself up into a ball and is doing a very good impression of being fast asleep.

FAREWELL FLAT 3

I'm in a sewer. It's dark, damp, wet and very smelly.
Grandma is standing next to me. 'Well, isn't this lovely?'
she says, turning and smiling at me. 'The perfect spot for
our new home. And nice and close to the Raticuses – so
convenient for playdates with Maximus!'

'I love playing with Stix,' I hear Maximus snarl, and turn
to see him standing behind us. His teeth are so long they
almost touch the floor.

Now I'm in the basement. I'm looking for Batz. I search
everywhere. I think I spot her hanging from a shelf. I rush

over, but she's not there. I hear her voice coming from near the filing cabinet, but when I get there she's not there either. 'Batz! Batz!' I cry out. 'Where are you? Why can't I find you?'

I wake in a cold, panicked sweat. It's possibly the worst night's sleep I have ever had. A small part of me hopes that us having to leave was a bad dream too. But as soon as Grandma speaks, I know it wasn't.

'Come on, my boy, it's time for us to get to the meeting,' she says, pulling me to my feet. 'The sooner we get on with this, the sooner we'll find a new home.'

I sense that she too is sad, but she's doing that grown-up thing of hiding it, putting on what the elders call a 'brave face'.

I'm pretty sure my face looks every bit how I feel: sad and all jumbled up. One day everything is fine, I'm eating pizza and going to school with my best friend; the next, Colin turns up and all of a sudden we're leaving – forced to go out into a world beyond Peewit Mansions, a scary place that I've never been to and where I'll have no friends.

I follow Grandma out of our nest in a daze. 'Goodbye,

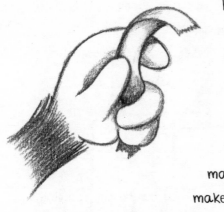

home,' I mutter tugging a shred of paper from it as I leave. I scrunch it up into a tight ball in my paw, determined to keep a small reminder.

'Goodbye, washing machine,' I whisper, as we make our way along the narrow path between it and the saucepan cupboard. I even bid farewell to the furry balls of dust that litter my path.

'Wow!' exclaims Grandma, as we step out into the kitchen. 'They sure pack fast.'

I let out a gasp of horror. The kitchen, as I knew it, is gone, replaced by a room of boxes, all stacked up and neatly labelled in black pen. There is even a small one with Trevor's name on it. For a moment I think they've packed him up too, but then I see him – fast asleep on his bed, wedged in next to a box labelled 'Saucepans/mugs/random stuff'.

I feel a sob rise up my throat. Our kitchen, the one I've grown up in, the one I learnt so much in, the one that has given me so many happy memories, is now just a pile of boxes. This **REALLY** is happening – no time at all to make any sense of it.

I notice Boo-Boo has drawn a picture on the side of one of the boxes. **A crayon drawing of her, Schnookums, MyLove and Trevor.** They all look very sad. If I could, I'd add a picture of myself and Grandma on there too, to complete the picture of the sad family who doesn't want to leave.

As I clamber up the kitchen drawers tears stream down my face, landing with a soft **splosh** on the floor beneath me.

The thought of never seeing my home again, or Boo-Boo, or Trevor, makes my heart actually ache.

How can Trevor be sleeping so soundly? Isn't he sad to be leaving too? I stare at him a while, hoping he'll wake up so I can say goodbye, but he doesn't, so I wave a silent goodbye in his direction.

'Come on!' calls Grandma, who seems to have found some food in the sink. 'The mans have had a curry. You should have some – this might be the last meal we get for a while.'

I slide down and find her licking at the remains of some sauce from a silver take-away container. Grandma loves spicy food.

I try and force down a grain or two of rice, but it's hopeless. My throat feels too raw.

Finally, it's time to leave. The time I've been dreading from the moment I woke up. Grandma takes my paw and we walk hand in hand to the middle of the sink. Without saying a word she tenderly kisses me on the top of my head and then wiggles herself down through the plughole.

I follow after her, leaving Flat 3 for the very last time.

GOODBYE, GRANDMA

By the time we reach the basement, a large group of elders, along with their young, have gathered on the tatty carpet in its centre. I spot Batz, sandwiched between some much larger bats: I guess it's her ma and pa and her brothers.

A large furry shape tunnels its way through the crowd and emerges in the middle. As it pulls itself up to its full height, I see it is a mole. A much larger, rounder version of Dug.

'Ah-hum,' says the mole, clapping his enormous muddy paws. 'Good folk of Peewit Mansions, if I may have your attention, please.' We all fall silent. 'Thank you for coming here tonight, for I know this is a meeting that none of us wanted to have, or ever thought we would have.'

The elders nod solemnly.

'But in Colin Royale we have finally met an adversary we cannot contain. Though believe me when I say we have tried. Thank you, Hazel and Lyudmila, for your efforts,' he says, nodding at Grandma and Dr Krapotkin. 'Colin is a mans hell-bent on turning our home into a place we cannot exist in. Something our Melvin can attest to, can you not, dear Melv?'

'Aye,' croaks Webbo's uncle, shakily raising a couple of legs.

'For this reason, the Committee of Elders has made the

difficult but necessary decision to evacuate the premises. It will now be down to each family to secure themselves a new, safe place to live. It is with the heaviest heart that I say this, as I will personally miss so many of the good friends I have made here.' He pauses, clasping his large paws in front of him and bowing his head. I look over at Batz, but instead catch the eye of one of her brothers, who I notice has a large bruise above his eye. He scowls back.

'It has also been decided,' the mole continues, drawing his head back up, 'that the young will stay here under the watchful and caring eye of Dr Krapotkin. She will look after them while we all go about the difficult task of securing our new homes. She has even gone so far as to modify the classroom – upgrading the wardrobe, with both an extra door and a special closing mechanism.'

He motions towards the wardrobe. In place of the missing door, there now hangs the door of the grandfather clock, held in place with a higgledy-piggledy collection of wooden planks.

Dr Krapotkin stands proudly at the back holding a

length of chain. She pulls this with a sharp tug, causing
the wardrobe's one original door to slam shut with a loud
BANG. Everyone jumps. Everyone, of course, but Grandma.

I guess she must have already known about all of this, probably even the bit about leaving without me.

'It's going to be OK,' she whispers, placing her paws gently on my shoulders. 'Your old grandma is an expert at home finding. I'll be back for you before you can say "stuffed-crust pizza".'

Finally, the mole announces it's time for us to say our goodbyes. And that's it. Just like that, I'm left saying farewell to her for the second time in my life. **The last time she promised she'd be right back too, only she got flushed down the toilet** (it's a long story). I desperately try not to think about this as I give her the biggest hug I can muster.

'Steady on,' she laughs.

'If you squeeze any tighter I'll pop.'

'I love you,' I mumble into her fur.

'I love you too, my boy,' she says, unwinding my arms from around her and looking at me earnestly. 'Now, you keep safe and promise me, **promise me you won't do anything silly, OK?'**

'OK.' I nod. I mean, what could I do anyway?

BATZ, SPATZ

I slowly make my way over to my classmates in the wardrobe, the tiny shred of nest gripped tightly in my paw as I clamber up the lampshade. It feels so similar to just a few days ago when school first started, only now everything is so different.

I let out a long, sad sigh.

'You **crying**, mini mouse?' sneers Maximus, his large body bumping past me and knocking me to the floor. As he spins round laughing, he spots the piece of nest I've dropped. He leaps down and snatches it up before I can reach it.

'What's this?' he says, giving it a sniff. 'Smells like a bit of filthy old mouse nest. Disgusting.' Gleefully he shreds it into even tinier pieces. I grit my teeth, fighting the urge to cry. He's just destroyed my last memory of home.

'Now, darlinks,' says Dr Krapotkin, as we all take our usual seats, 'before I explain what we shall be doing next, I have a very quick question for Maximus.'

'Better make sure it's an easy one,' I hear Batz giggle. I would laugh if I wasn't so angry.

'As a member of the subterranean sewer-dwelling set, your family is exempt from Colin's development – no mans is going to go and clean up down there. Which means, darlink, you are free to go. You do not need to be here in my care. You can return to your parents.'

'Oh,' says Maximus, clearly taken by surprise.
'I, err ... OK.'

We all turn to look at him. He doesn't seem very keen to go anywhere.

'Of course, you can choose to stay here with us if you like, darlink,' says Dr Krapotkin, 'but I just needed to give you the choice.'

'I, err ... think I'll stay here,' he says, then adding under his breath too quietly for Dr Krapotkin to hear, 'with you bunch of total losers.'

Huh, I think. He must REALLY not like his parents if he'd rather hang out with us.

'OK, great news,' says Dr Krapotkin giving Maximus a big smile. 'Now, darlinks, for these last few days together, our main focus will be the business of survival.'

'S-survival?' stammers Dug. 'I-I thought we were going to be safe here with you?'

'And you will be, darlink ... there is no reason what-so-ever for Colin to come down here. I cannot see how the basement fits into his plans. However, the key here is not to be complacent. This old battle bird has seen first-hand what happens when you don't give the enemy the respect they deserve – may the soul of dear Mr Krapotkin rest in peace. And may that pesky cat, Fluffy, rot in hell!' she says gravely. 'I shall not let a mistake like that happen again. We shall be vigilant to a potential breach of our position day and night and night and day. We shall, darlinks, be keeping all of our eyes permanently peeled!'

'But we can't zzzzztay awake alwayzzz,' buzzes Blue. 'That would be impozzzzible.'

'Indeed, that is why, darlinks, you are going to pair up and take it in turns to be on watch. You will use my paint tin as your viewing platform. If you see anything suspicious or untoward you will alert me immediately. And when you are not on watch, I want you resting – should we have any unexpected visitors, I need you all as sharp as pointy arrows. Now, team up and get to it.'

Of course, I team up with Batz. We are third on 'watch' after Dug and Webbo and Blue and Underlay. I curl myself up in the corner of the wardrobe and, just like Dr Krapotkin instructed, try and get some rest. But, even though I feel tired, I can't sleep. My mind won't stop whirring.

'Hey! How you doing?' I hear Batz whisper, and look up

to see her standing over me. Clearly she can't sleep either, unlike Maximus, who is out like a light next to me, snoring like MyLove.

'I'm sad,' I admit. 'Sad I'm going to lose all my friends, sad I'm not going to see you any more.'

'Hey, don't worry about it!' she says, her face breaking into a broad grin. 'It's going to be fine, you'll see!' How can she look happy about something so depressing? Maybe Maximus was right and she doesn't want to be my friend any more? Maybe she won't even miss me?

'You seem to be taking it all very well.' I try to sound as casual as I can. 'I mean, it doesn't feel like something to smile about to me.'

'Err, I dunno, I guess I've got a naturally happy face. I'm just trying to stay positive.' She shrugs as if she couldn't care less either way.

Or maybe it's because you're excited about the possibility of finding a new best friend, I think, but I don't say it. I don't really know what to say. 'Well, I, err ... I guess ... but it's hard to feel positive right now when we, you know, have to find a new home and stuff.'

'Oh, come on,' she says, rolling her eyes. 'Stop being such a mouse!'

'What do you mean by that?' I scowl.

'You know, being all over the top and dramatic.' She laughs, flapping her wings madly.

'Well, YOU should stop being such a bat,' I snap back. 'Being all ... all big-mouthed and STUPID.'

'Wow! I mean w-OW!' she says, placing her wings on her hips. She looks at me with such an expression of hurt, I almost regret what I said. Clearly I've struck a nerve. But then, she did start it. So why should I feel bad? 'Well, now I know just how you feel about me ...' she continues, 'maybe it's for the best that we won't be friends any more.'

'I agree!' I snap.

We glower at each other, then Batz flies back up to her perch, and

I'm left alone.

'Stix and Batz ... you're up

next!' It's Dr Krapotkin, waving us over to the paint pot.
'Good work, Underlay and Blue,' she says, ushering them
down. 'Now you two, no clowning around. I know you like
to have a laugh and all that, but you need to put your
serious heads on, OK, darlinks?'

'Oh, he's got his serious head on all
right,' mumbles
Batz, as we
take our seat
on the lid of
the tin. 'His
seriously rude
head.'

**'You
started it,'** I
growl, sitting
down with my
back to her.

We sit in
stony silence
staring out

across the basement. I'm so angry, but I'm also so sad. I wish we hadn't said all those things. I wish we were still friends. I glance across at her and am about to say something, but I don't get the chance because right then we both hear the faint sound of footsteps coming down the stairs, followed by a key being turned in the basement door, followed by ...

... **THE DOOR CREAKING OPEN.**

BLUE, NO!

In the gloom, I can just make out two figures standing in
the doorway. One is a big, burly mans, wearing a pair of
overalls, the other is unmistakably ...

'Colin!' I whisper. 'The bad mans. That's him!' In his arms
he is carrying the Duchess.

'Come on, we've got to tell Krapotkin,' says Batz, leaping
down off the tin.

'And this wretched filth-hole is the basement,' Colin
is saying as he strides down the stairs. 'Some little critter
chewed through the electrics, so I'm afraid we'll have
to view it by torchlight.' A beam of light sweeps across
the room.

'Dr Krapotkin! Dr Krapotkin!' we whisper, shaking her
awake.

'What is it, Sergeant Major? Time to release the big
guns?' she squawks, coming to with a start. As soon as
she sees us and realises what's going on, she leaps to her
good foot.

'It's Colin,' I whisper urgently, pointing at the roving torch beam. 'He's in the basement!'

'Right, if you could just put the bag of Mummy's old clothes over there,' we hear Colin say, 'and hide that hideous portrait of her somewhere, then we can get down to business.'

'Very good, guv'nor,' says the burly mans, slinging a bin liner and a large gold-framed picture next to a big box of old magazines. 'Now, am I right in finkin' this is where you're wanting the testin' area?'

'Testing area?' mutters Dr Krapotkin, sounding rather perplexed. 'Never heard of that in a block of flats.'

'That's right,' replies Colin. 'I'm thinking the main area will be around here.' He illuminates the filing cabinet with his torch. 'And over here,' he says, swinging the beam towards us. 'The waste and disposal units ...'

Quick as a flash, Dr Krapotkin reaches for the chain. She gives it a yank and with a loud BANG the wardrobe door swings shut, waking everyone inside.

Colin lets out a frightened yelp. **'What was that?'** he squeaks. 'Did that wardrobe door just close on its own?'

'You know, I've 'eard it said that these old blocks are 'aunted,' says the big, burly mans, his voice dropping to almost a whisper. 'Perhaps there's a ghost down 'ere? The spirit of a past resident.'

'G-ghosts?' stammers Colin. 'Really? You believe in all that?'

'Oh, yeah, my old nan haunts our place for sure — wailing away all night, keeping us up. You can knock off pests with poisons and potions, but ain't nothing that can get rid of an angry spirit.'

'It's not ghosts, you bone-headed buffoons,' I hear the Duchess yap.

'Yes, well, I think we're done here, let's go,' replies Colin, clearly a little shaken.

We all rush forwards and press our faces against the thin gap between the two doors and watch as he walks back towards the stairs clutching a wriggling Duchess tightly in his arms.

'Phew!' whispers Webbo. 'Saved by the door.'

But just as they reach the bottom of the stairs, with one final wiggle, the Duchess manages to free herself from his arms. She drops to the floor with a soft thud.

'It's not time to go just yet,' she yaps.

And with that she bounds across the floor towards us.

'She's such a free-spirit,' laughs Colin nervously. 'Well, I guess this gives us a moment to talk about the kind of security locks I want on the doors.'

'Where are you? Where are you?' whispers the Duchess, sniffing the air. 'You can't hide from me.'

'Don't move a muscle, darlinks,' commands Dr Krapotkin.

A tiny part of me hopes the Duchess is looking for someone else. But as she reaches the wardrobe and looks up, it's clear exactly who she's after.

We all stand, frozen with fear.

Even Maximus looks scared.

'Hmmm.' She sniffs. 'I'm getting a hint of pigeon, a waft of rat, of bat, of mole ... a tang of spider, the musty musk of a carpet beetle and is that ... the faint aroma of ... mouse?'

'And therezzz me azzzzwell!' buzzes Blue, clearly hurt at being left out.

'And how could I have missed the odorous pong of a filthy house fly?' The Duchess smirks, flashing a set of sharp pointy teeth. 'Now, you little dirt bags, here's the thing. As you may have gathered, Colin's pretty keen on getting rid of the likes of you — loves his poisons, does our Col — it's all about the chemicals for him. Whereas I, being a more enlightened creature, am much more ... organic. I'm more interested in the raw killing experience, you know, the chase, the fight — all that **real animal** stuff. What it boils down to' — she slowly licks her grinning lips — 'is that I'm a dog with a thirst for blood.'

'Don't worry, darlinks,' whispers Dr Krapotkin, 'she can't get to us in here.'

'Well, "darlinks", that's not strictly true. You see, you

either play ball, or I call Colin over, and I'm telling you, it won't be pretty.'

'Dogs can't talk to mans,' I whisper. 'Trevor tries it all the time and it never works.'

'Oh, doesn't it?' says the Duchess with a grin, her hearing clearly much better than I anticipated. 'Trevor couldn't train a monkey to eat bananas. Clever me, on the other paw, has spent years teaching my mans to do just as I command. Just watch this.'

She lets out a strange little howl and Colin immediately stops mid-conversation. 'What is it, Duchy-poo?' he says, looking over.

'Ignore the pet name thing,' she sighs. 'It's next on my list of things to train him NOT to do. Now, watch this,' she says, and lets out a series of short, sharp yaps.

'There's something you want me to see in the wardrobe?' replies Colin.

I can't believe it. He really can understand her.

'OK, OK,' gulps Dr Krapotkin. 'Make him stop, tell us what you want. We are all ears, darlink.'

The Duchess emits another short little howl. This time Colin stops in his tracks, turns and goes back to chatting with the burly mans. Quite unbelievable!

'What I want,' she beams, 'is to play a little game. It's called ... Battle Royale – get it? Colin Royale, Battle Royale ... Oh, never mind, I doubt you're clever enough for word play. Anyway, it goes like this ... One at a time you each battle me ... fun, huh? And we keep on going until one of you beats me ... which won't happen, but don't worry about that. All you've got to concern yourselves with is being good sports and playing along.' She gnashes her teeth excitedly. 'Oh, this is going to be so enjoyable. Who wants to go first? And someone HAS to go first ... otherwise I'll call back Chemical Col.'

'Th-this is preposterous, darlink,' blurts Dr Krapotkin.

'You can't fight them. They are just children.'

'Even juicier,' replies the Duchess, grinning and licking her lips. 'Now, come on. I'll give you five seconds before I get Mr Spray-and-Slay over. **Five ... four ... three ...**'

I hear a loud buzz of wings.

'**... two ...**'

Above me, Blue squeezes himself out of the small gap between the doors. '**I've got this guyzzzz,**' he calls. '**She'll**

never catch me. I'm too fazzzzt.'

We watch in stunned silence as he flies out and starts zooming around her.

'Nazzty dog. Can't catch me!' he taunts, flying faster and faster. 'I'll zzend your head into a zzzzpin.'

'Wanna bet?' growls the Duchess, her head whipping around and around as her eyes try desperately to follow him.

'Stop it! Stop it, you foul beast!' cries Dr Krapotkin, throwing herself at the two doors, trying to force her way through the slender gap.

'I'm Blue the zzzzzzuper fly,' Blue goads.

He seems be getting the better of her. Surely she can't keep this up for much longer, she must be getting dizzy. And then, suddenly, she stops. She stands stock-still as Blue circles her once more.

'These blasted doors!' screeches Dr Krapotkin, still throwing herself against them. 'Why won't they open?' She hits them with all her might and there's a mighty crack, but it's not the wood. It's her wing. She falls to the floor, her left wing twisted at a very strange angle.

I look back at Blue just in time to see him whizz towards the Duchess's nose.

'Zzzzzzilly dog, you looozzzzzzz.' He laughs. 'I winzzzzz.'

But, quick as a flash, just as he passes over the tip, the Duchess flicks her head up and – SNAP! – catches him in her jaws. She swallows loudly and licks her lips.

And that's that.

One moment he's there, the next ... he's gone.

RUB OUT THE RULE BOOK

'Mmmmmm, crunchy and a little bit salty,' says the Duchess, smiling. 'I can't wait to see what the next one of you tastes like.'

'What's going on? What was all that banging and screeching?' calls a panicked Colin from the other side of the basement. 'Come on, Duchess, I don't want to spend a moment longer down here.'

'See you again very soon for the next round,' she calls back over her shoulder, as she bounces over to him.

'Let's get out of this foul place,' Colin says, scooping the

Duchess up in his arms and kissing her on the top of her head. 'We need to get to the shops before they close – buy some bleach to clean off that nasty stain Mummy's stupid portrait left on the living-room wall.'

And with that the door slams shut and they are gone.

We all stand in stony, stunned silence, none of us knowing what to do or what to say. Blue, poor Blue – gone, just like that.

I look at the empty spot where he used to sit. I think of him buzzing around my head, making me dizzy, making me laugh.

'Oh, Blue,' sobs Dug, finally. 'Oh, how terrible.'

'I mean, I'm as partial to a fly as the next spider,' says Webbo sadly, 'but not Blue. Man ... he was a total legend.'

Even Maximus looks sad.

'Idon'twanthertotakeanotheroneofus!' gabbles Underlay

nervously, clasping the tiny
shred of rug she calls her
'comfort carpet' tightly
between her claws.

CRASH!

From behind us comes the loud slam of metal hitting
wood. We all spin round. It's Dr Krapotkin, she's kicked over
the old paint pot.

'AND I WON'T LET HER! NO! NO! NO!' she screeches. 'I shall
not let this little dislocation' – she
nods down at her injured left
wing, which is horribly
twisted, like
someone has put it
on the wrong way
around – 'prevent
me from protecting
you. I shall not see
another of my pupils
murdered. I SHALL NOT,
WILL NOT AND CANNOT!'

As she says this, she frantically rubs, with her good right wing, at the one rule she chalked on the classroom blackboard only a couple of nights ago. 'This rule was to keep you safe from Colin. I hadn't counted on his pet being a murderous devil-dog with her own agenda. So now I am not just tearing up the rule book – I'm rubbing it out and creating a new one!'

1. **REVENGE**
2. **REVENGE**
3. **REVENGE**
4. **REVENGE**
5. **REVENGE**

... she scrawls in large letters.

'The gloves are coming off, darlinks.' She reaches her good wing down and dabs it into the little puddle of red paint that has dribbled out of the overturned paint tin. Then proudly draws the anarchic 'A' back on her chest. 'We must punish that vile hound for eating Blue – and we must do it swiftly, before she takes another one of us!'

'B-but h-how?' stammers a wide-eyed Dug.

'A snake cannot live without its head, just as a dog cannot be without its owner. If Colin goes then so does she — that is the rule when you are a domesticated pet.' She spits the words 'domesticated' and 'pet' like she is trying to clear dirt from her beak. 'We shall unleash upon him a pestilence like never before. We shall not just bother him —

we shall traumatise him out of the building ... we shall take being a pest to whole new level! Yes, it will be **unbelievably dangerous.** Yes, it will take every ounce of skill we possess. But, it's us or the dog, darlinks.'

'But pests aren't allowed in Flat 5,' says Webbo.

'That was then, darlink, this is now. Doris no longer lives there. So that's another rule we can rip up. The only problem we've got is that none of us have ever been up there, which means we are going to need to do some sneaking and some peeking before we can make a plan. So, we shall conduct "reconnaissance", darlinks,' she declares authoritatively. 'We will send in a small team to ascertain the strategic features, carry out observations and locate the enemy. Cunning plans are nothing without careful planning.'

We all nod furiously; though I really have no idea what Dr Kraptokin is going on about. But it doesn't matter. The sadness I feel in my heart about losing Blue, about losing our home, and the stomach-churning fear I feel about the Duchess returning is suddenly lifted by the idea of being able to do something about it.

The elders wouldn't, but **we will!**

'And we have been given the perfect window of opportunity,' she continues. 'Colin has gone to the shops. So let's get a team up there A-S-A-P while it's safe. I shall be Commandant, Webbo, darlink, you will be my number two. I want you to make use of all four of your eyes – work out what is what and where is where. Maximus, you'll be the muscle, darlink – anything goes wrong, you'll be the first line of defence.'

'What?' says Maximus, looking momentarily horrified. 'I mean, yeah, right, not a problem. I beat up dogs for fun.'

'Liar, liar, tail on fire.' I hear the Plagues giggle from somewhere near his ear.

'And you, Stix,' she says turning to me, 'I want you using that agility, darlink ...'

'Err, right. No problem,' I say, as calmly as I can, but my heartbeat is suddenly rocketing. I mean, I want to do something, I really do, but the idea of going into the flat of two crazed pest-killers ...

'Figure out where the hidey-holes are, where we can mount our attacks from. And Batz?' she says. Batz looks up nervously. 'You'll be his wing man, darlink – get up there, do some aerial scouting. Any questions?'

Batz and I glance at each other briefly, then look away again.

'Underlay and Dug, your job is to stay down here, safe and hidden and keep an eye on the place.' They both nod furiously. I really like the sound of their jobs! 'OK, now if you will follow me ...' She grabs her injured wing and, with a painful sounding clunk, twists it round the right way. 'I will show you the hidden highway to Flat number 5.'

She leads us to a small crumbling hole, behind a pile of old paint cans. The oldest looking cobwebs in the world cover the entrance.

'Looks like the works of my great, great grandma,' says Webbo, as Dr Krapotkin reaches forward to clear them away.

'Flaming rings of firey pain!' she screeches, recoiling in agony.

'Wing injuries take time to heal,' says Batz compassionately. 'Look, I'm sure we can do this on our own – the flat's empty after all.'

'Absolutely not, Darlink!' She grimaces. 'I shall not let a

little pain hold me ba—'

But she doesn't get to finish, because just then we hear a horribly familiar sound.

The basement door.

'Everybody HIDE!' she squawks herding us all into the cramped tunnel opening. The door creaks open.

Then I hear it: the unmistakable soft pad of dog paws making their way down the basement stairs.

My blood turns to ice. The Duchess has come back!

We desperately try to press ourselves further back into the hole, stacking ourselves in an uncomfortable jumble: me on Maximus, Batz on top of me and Webbo on top of her. Dr Krapotkin is squashed up against us all, blocking the entrance. We're packed so tight we can hardly breathe.

Pad

Pad

Pad

She's coming straight for us.

Pad

Pad

Pad

The paws get closer.

Pad

Pad

Pad

I hear her sniff; she's right outside. What are we going to do? We're jammed in too tight to move – **we're trapped!** Beneath me I feel Maximus trembling.

She sniffs again.

'You will not take another of my pupils,' cries Dr Krapotkin launching herself out of the tunnel entrance. 'No ... no ... no ... over my dead body!'

There's a loud WUMPH! Followed by another and another.

'Take that! And that! And that!' I hear Dr Krapotkin screech over the frantic sound of flapping feathers. 'You murderous beast! You ...' She stops suddenly, and everything goes quiet. 'Wait, you're not ...'

And then I hear a whimper ... a faint, but familiar whimper ... It's not the Duchess, it's ...

TREVOR!!!

'**TREVOR!**' I blurt, tumbling out of the tunnel, Batz, Webbo and Maximus crashing after me. 'STOP, Dr Krapotkin, it's OK, it's just Trevor!'

'Trevor?' replies Dr Krapotkin breathlessly.

Poor Trevor looks terrified as he points a trembling paw at me. 'Yes, I looking for mouse,' he says. 'I want speak with him.'

'He's the dog I live with,' I explain.

'That may be, darlink, but dogs are no friend of ours,' declares Dr Krapotkin. 'They are not to be trusted.'

I look at Trevor; his pleading eyes stare back. 'Please help,' he whimpers.

I think back to the other night, how he didn't hurt me, even though he could have.

'He's not as dangerous as he looks,' I say. 'He's just a bit ... grumpy.'

'Hmmm,' says Dr Krapotkin, eyeing him this time with her small eye. 'So then, dog, what are you doing down here?'

'Trevor not like smelly mans and rude dog. Trevor want them gone. Trevor want P.E.S.T.S. to do something.'

'You know about us?' I ask.

'All creatures know about us, darlink ... but, much as they would like, not all creatures can be us – especially not dogs,' she says pointedly. 'Dogs are too busy sucking up to the mans to bother them like we pests do.

However, dog, you will be pleased to hear we are planning on doing something.'

'But you injured,' says Trevor, nodding at Dr Krapotkin's now exceedingly limp wing. 'Maybe Trevor can help?' He beams.

'Oh, dude,' laughs Webbo, 'that's a funny one. You're mans' best friend! What are you going to do, lick Colin to death?'

'Yeah!' chips in Maximus who, I notice, has partially hidden himself behind the bookshelf. From his fur, I can hear the Plagues moaning about the smell of Trevor's flea collar.

'OK, dog,' says Dr Krapotkin, releasing him from her stare, 'in normal times I would usually be agreeing with my pupils. But in this special circumstance you may be of use. It would make me feel a whole lot better about sending them off, alone, on their little "recon" mission, if I knew they had a look-out guy. Think you can be that dog, Rover? Hang outside Flat 5, woof twice if Colin comes back early?'

'Oh, yes, yes.' Trevor nods fervently. 'Trevor be good doorbell.'

'Great. So now let's get the rest of you back in that hidden highway.' She smiles.

'Err, I think I'll look for a window or a vent and see you all up there,' says Batz, clearly not so keen after her last experience.

'Very well, and don't forget, Darlinks, I want you all to stay as focused as a pair of expensive binoculars. I want a full report of what's up there, darlinks,' says Dr Krapotkin. 'We need to know the lie of the land and, by my calculations, you have no more than not very long at all, so get going!'

FLAT 5

The climb is long and hard. We keep having to stop to remove small chunks of brick that have fallen and blocked our path. It's clear no creature has been up here for a very long time. Maximus, being the largest, struggles the most.

'Come on, you big lump,' I hear Plague One tease.

'Shouldn't have eaten that whole pack of mouldy doughnuts,' mocks Plague Two.

Finally, we reach the end of our torturous climb and find ourselves staring at the back of an air vent. An overpowering, pungent smell of bleach wafts through from the other side. I fight desperately not to sneeze. We gather at the slats and peer out nervously. On the other side of the vent is a hallway. A very white, bright and shiny hallway. I listen intently, but all I can hear is my own heartbeat and Maximus's heavy breathing.

The window on the opposite wall rattles, making us all jump.

'Argh, it's the stupid bat,' curses Maximus. Sure enough I look up and see Batz. She's using her wings to push up the bottom half of the window; from the strain on her face it looks like a tough job. Finally, it slides up and she swoops in.

'Got to love a cantilevered sash-window,' she says gliding down to the vent. 'Come on, what you waiting for?'

As we scamper down the hallway, it quickly becomes apparent we have a **VERY** big problem. Colin's flat is ... empty. It's so unbelievably clean and tidy, that there doesn't appear to be any furniture, any stuff.

How are we going to be pesty? There's no stuff to knock

over, no cables to gnaw through and nothing to scratch or scurry around.

'**Atchoo!**' I sneeze loudly as we enter the kitchen. 'ATCHOO! ATCHOO! ATCHOO!' The smell of cleaning products is overwhelming.

'Jeez,' says Webbo, covering his mouth. 'How could anyone live in this kind of stench? It's totally **pong-mungous.**'

'Yeah, it's completely **whiff-tastic,**' says Batz, looping around the room.

'**Utterly reeky-deeky,**' continues Webbo. Batz hi-fives him and they both giggle.

'Aww, seems the bat's got a new best friend. Dumped you and moved on to the spider,' whispers Maximus, placing a heavy paw on my shoulder.

I shift away from his grasp, determined not to show the crushing jealously I suddenly feel. 'Right,' I say cheerily. 'I'm going to get on and see what we can do.'

I try to climb up to the kitchen countertop to see what's there, but the kitchen's made of a shiny white material and there are no handles to grip on to, so I just slide back down again. No matter how hard I try, I can't get up there.

'Oh, boy, this is going to be a tough place to get pesty,' says Webbo, echoing my thoughts.

'There's not even a pendant light to rattle,' Batz announces disappointedly, circling above us.

I try and dig my claws into the floorboards, to see if I can make a noise that way, but they are rock hard.

'High gloss varnish,' says Webbo. 'You ain't gonna get a peep out of those babies.'

There's nowhere to scratch and scrabble, to gnaw or chew.

'I could take a dump in the microwave,' declares Maximus proudly.

'And how are you going to get up there?' asks Batz. 'Grow a pair of wings?'

'OK, let's try the bedroom,' says Webbo. 'Perhaps we'll get lucky there.'

But the bedroom is even worse than the kitchen. There is nothing in it but a large, perfectly-made bed with an enormous picture of the Duchess hanging above it. Her cruel coal-black eyes stare back at me, sending an icy chill down my spine. I never want to see her again. Ever.

'Fur-reaky painting,' declares Batz. 'Geddit? **Fur**-reaky!'

'Fu-unny,' giggles Webbo, and they both burst out laughing.

'Aww, they're made for each other,' whispers Maximus,

nudging me so hard I almost fall over.

'Come on,' I say, pretending not to have heard him. 'We haven't been to the living room yet. Maybe we'll find something there.'

But as we walk in we are met by a strange and unexpected sight. The room is filled with boxes all neatly stacked one on top of the other, all the way up to the ceiling. There's hardly any room for Colin's TV and sofa. However, these aren't packed full of household stuff like the ones in MyLove and Schnookums's kitchen. These are boxes full of ...

'Great webs of fire!' gasps Webbo.

'O.M.G.G.G.G.,' gulps Batz.

On every box is a picture of Colin's grinning face giving a big thumbs up. Under which are printed the words PEST CONTROL WITH THE ROYALE SEAL OF EXCELLENCE.

My mouth drops open as I read the descriptions:

Royale's Mega Mouse Traps

Royale's Spider Slayer

Royale's Bat-Be-Gone Repellent

Royale's Bug Obliterator

Royale's Rat Eradicator

Royale's Pigeon Poison

He doesn't just like to kill us — he also makes the stuff to kill us with.

'I feel sick,' says Webbo.

'You'll feel even worse once you see this,' says Batz, pointing at a huge sheet of paper stuck on the wall.

It's a map of the block. Across the top in large letters it says: 'Royale's Pesticide Emporium — Expansion Plans Stage One.'

I look at the flats, only instead of being labelled 1, 2, 3 and 4 they are now marked as Production Stations.

'L-l-look,' says Webbo, pointing two trembling legs at Flat 4. 'SPIDER SLAYER MANUFACTURE,' I read. That must have been the strange machines I saw in Tarquin's flat the other night!

I look at Flat 3. It's labelled, RAT/MOUSE POISON DISTILLATION.

'And it gets even worse. Look at the basement.' Batz points at the bottom of the picture. 'LIVE SPECIMEN TESTING LABORATORY,' she reads, her voice quivering.

To my horror I see the basement has been divided up

into separate areas: Mouse testing/Bug testing/Spider testing …

I suddenly feel faint – I can't read any more.

'We've got to get out of here NOW,' says Webbo, all four of his eyes wide with fear. 'There is no way we can pest this mans out.'

But just as we are making our way across the room we hear Trevor go yapping mad.

WEBBO, WATCH OUT!

'**Woof! Woof! Woof! Woof! Woof!**' barks Trevor.

'Dr Krapotkin said two for danger,' says Webbo stopping in his tracks. 'What does five mean?'

'It means,' I say listening to the sound of mans feet striding down the hallway towards the living room, 'he barked too late!'

Fast as we can, Webbo, Maximus and I dart behind a stack of boxes. Batz hides herself in the folds of a curtain.

'Shut up, Mutley, and shove off back to the swampy flat where you belong.' I hear the Duchess growl at Trevor.

But I don't hear Trevor's reply, because just at that moment Colin walks into the living room. He places the

bucket of water he is carrying on the floor and pulls out a scrubbing brush.

'Just look at the horrible marks your portrait has left, Mummy,' he mutters angrily, scrubbing at a square yellow stain on the wall identical in shape and size to the painting he left in the basement earlier. 'It's like I just ... can't ... get ... rid ... of ... you,' he puffs.

Surely this is our chance to escape.

'Come on,' I whisper. 'Let's get out of here while he's distracted.'

Fast as we can, we sprint out of the living room. But as we round the corner into the hallway our hearts stop.

It's the Duchess, blocking our path. **'Well, well, well!** What are you doing here? Oh, I know, you've come for round two.' She winks, her cold eyes glinting evilly. 'Soooo, who wants to go next? Shall we say ... the spider? Do it in size order ... keep the tastiest till last.' She smiles at

Maximus, who takes a step back, making a strange sound like a deflating balloon.

'Come on, spidey ...' She turns her attention back to Webbo. 'I'll show you how I really fight ... you've not seen anything yet! Ha! Ha! Ha!'

'Do something, Maximus!' I hiss.

'I ... err ... I'm ...' he stammers. 'I'm scared of dogs, all right!' And with that he turns and runs across the hallway and tries frantically to scramble back into the air vent. But he gets stuck halfway, leaving his bottom and back legs wiggling in mid-air. If we weren't in such a dangerous situation, I'd laugh.

The Duchess pays no attention. All her focus is on Webbo. 'You box with the right legs or the left? Orthodox or southpaw?' she pants, bobbing left to right.

Webbo makes a run for the air vent too, but the Duchess is fast, scarily fast. Quick as a flash she catches him, pinning one of his legs to the floor with her paw.

'Tut! Tut! Running away, that's against the rules.' She frowns. 'For that I'm going to have to remove your legs ... starting with this one.'

'No ... no ... please, no,' whimpers Webbo, his eyes brimming with tears.

I've got to do something. The Duchess's bottom wiggles excitedly as she starts tugging on Webbo's leg. **That's it**, I think, and without a moment to consider the stupidity of what I'm doing, I launch myself at her bum. It's just like the game I play with Trevor, only the challenge here is most definitely to land on it.

I hit it dead on, grabbing hold of two large clumps of her fur with my front paws. I yank them apart and then drive my teeth into the pink flesh beneath.

'What the ...?' She howls, spinning round and round, trying to see what has caused her the pain, but she can't see me as my teeth are still clamped to her bottom. As I whizz around with her I catch a blurry glimpse of Batz. She swoops down, picks up the stunned Webbo and flies out of the window.

'Well, I suppose we can make it a tag-team event,' snarls the Duchess, spinning faster still, her snapping teeth getting closer and closer. I start to lose my grip. I can't hold on any longer. Before I know it, I'm flying through the air. I slam into something soft and hairy. Maximus's bottom! The force shoves him through the vent.

I fall to the floor and look up just in time to see the Duchess bounding towards me. Quick as a flash I leap to my feet and scramble after Maximus.

'No! No! No!' she shrieks, pressing her nose through the metal slats. 'I'll make you pay for your cowardliness. I'll make you PAY!'

'Duchess! Duchess!' I hear Colin cry. 'What's going on? Who's out here with you?'

'It's just pests,' she snarls angrily.

A gust of wind catches the open window. It falls shut with a loud bang.

'What the ...? Who opened the window?' Colin shrieks, leaping up in the air. 'Surely the builder's wrong, it can't be a ghost. Though I was just saying some not very nice things to Mummy ... But it can't be ... can it?'

'Of course it's not, you perma-tanned nincompoop,' replies the Duchess angrily.

But this time Colin clearly doesn't understand her.

SUPER-DUPER-STITIOUS

I land with a heavy thud at the bottom of the hidden highway, my heart still pounding.

Webbo so nearly got all his legs pulled off, and for what? To find that it's impossible to bother Colin out and that his plans for the mansion block are worse than we could ever have imagined.

Above me I see Batz soar across the basement and over to the wardrobe, depositing a traumatised-looking Webbo back in his place next to Dug.

'What's going on?' asks a shocked Dr Krapotkin. 'What happened, Webbo?'

'The mans and the dog came back,' says Batz. 'Someone forgot to warn us in time!'

'Err ... Trevor very sorry about that,' he says humbly. 'Got distracted by daydream about old bone.'

'And where is Stix?' squawks Dr Krapokin. 'Please don't say he caught him?'

'No, no, I'm here. I'm fine,' I say, leaping off the end of the lampshade.

'Yeah, I helped him escape,' says Maximus, lying through his huge yellow teeth.

I open my mouth to protest, but Maximus continues before I can get a word out.

'And we discovered what Colin is really up to: he's turning Peewit Mansions into a factory – a factory that makes pesticides!'

'What?!' squawks Dr Krapotkin, her small eye becoming almost the same size as her big one.

'Yeah,' says Batz. 'And the basement is going to be where

he does his testing to see if his horrible products work.'

'**Great falcon claws!!**' blusters Dr Krapotkin.

'He's Nuke-A-Pest times a hundred-million,' says Webbo, pulling himself unsteadily to his feet. 'And there's no way we can stop him, or get rid of the Duchess. There is nothing in Flat 5 for us to use to bother him. It's too clean and tidy.'

'This is beyond a disaster! Oh, if only Doris hadn't up and popped her clogs,' Dr Krapotkin wails, punching the side of the wardrobe with her good wing. 'If she were here, none of this would be happening.'

I think back to Colin a moment ago – panicking that he had somehow upset the ghost of his Ma. My brain begins to whirr ...

'**Maybe she can return!**' I cry.

'**What, you gonna bring her back from the dead?**' asks Maximus with a smirk.

'No, we are going to BE her,' I say, pacing the wardrobe floor as my thoughts start to take shape in my head. 'Just now, Colin mistook the window Batz left open and the sound of us fighting for some kind of ghostly goings-on. He thinks Doris has come back to tell him off or something. He was terrified.'

'Ah-hah!' cries Dr Krapotkin. 'He's superstitious!'

'Yeah, he's totally superstupidous,' says Maximus, laughing and pointing at me.

'She said **superstitious**,' says Webbo, rolling all four eyes. 'And she meant **Colin**, you numbskull.'

'He's not afraid of pests. But he's definitely afraid of ghosts,' I say excitedly, as I realise what I've stumbled on. 'We can't pest him out in the traditional way ... but we can use our skills to SPOOK him out!'

'Yes! Yes!' Dr Krapotkin claps awkwardly with her good wing. 'We shall use super-advanced skills to trick him. Doris would never have approved of what he's done, so we shall make him believe beyond a doubt that she really has come back to show him how cross she is. This is a most brilliant piece of thinking, Stix!'

Trevor shuffles himself over and sits next to me. We must look a funny pair, me so small and him so big.

'Mouse do much better than Trevor,' he says. 'Mouse got little head, but big brain.'

'Thanks, Trevor.' I laugh, realising this is the first proper conversation I have ever really had with him.

I sense someone watching us and look up to see Batz. She scowls and looks away. Maybe she does still care?

'Now all we need to do is work out how to execute this horrible haunting, and then we shall strike! And when I say strike, darlinks, I mean tonight. At midnight. Whilst the iron is, as they say, exceptionally hot.'

GHOSTLY
BEGINNINGS

'OK, listen up!' says Dr Krapotkin, pulling out her lump of chalk. 'Time to make the BIG plan of action. Gigantic problems call for epic solutions. We are going to be using a.d.v.a.n.c.e.d. skills, darlinks — it's going to be super difficult and super dangerous. But I believe in you. We CAN do this.' She writes a neat list on the blackboard.

1. Unexplained temperature change.
2. Strange technological glitches.
3. Unusual smells.

4. Unexplained object movement or unidentifiable sounds.

5. Feeling of being touched by unseen hands.

'Righty right, darlinks. These are the things which will make Colin believe the building is haunted. So here's my thinkings: Batz, you cover off point one. We are coming into the winter time, so it's nice and cold at night – open a few windows, find the thermostat and turn it down, make the place chilly – think you can do that?'

'Indeedy-do.' Batz nods.

'Maximus, you're in charge of point two. Locate the main electrical fuse box. Nibble a cable or two – but do not, I repeat, **DO NOT bite through them**. I just want some flickering lights, not a blackout. OK?'

'OK,' he says, rolling his eyes.

'Now, unusual smells – this one's for you, Underlay. Lucky for us Colin dumped that bag of Doris's old clothes down here. I want you to find something that really smells of her, then chew it into tiny shreds. Once we're in the flat, scatter it around. I want the place smelling like she's back.'

'Noproblemoldladysmellscomingrightup!' says Underlay
excitedly.

'On to number four – Stix, I want objects moving,
things switching on and off. For this we are going to need
to get you up to the electrical appliances on the kitchen
countertop – Batz, I want you there to give him a helping
wing if he needs it. This is going to put you out in the
open. So, the key here, darlink, is not to be seen. Make sure
whatever you do, you keep yourself hidden. Got it?'

'Yup. Sure thing,' I say calmly, which is completely at
odds with the panic I feel on hearing the words, 'out in the
open'. A mouse **NEVER** wants to be out in the open when a
mans is around. Especially not a mans like Colin, who has a
dog like the Duchess!

'Now, on to the feeling of being touched. Webbo, think
you can handle this, darlink? Put those long, hairy legs to
work?'

'You m-mean I've gotta TOUCH the dude?' says Webbo
nervously.

'Yes, darlink. I want you to be the one to wake him up,
kick this whole thing off.'

'It's all right, he won't have a can of bug spray in his bed,' I whisper.

'You wanna bet?' replies Webbo, all four of his eyebrows furrowing into a wiggly line of concern.

'I've got an idea,' whispers Dug, his eyes wide with excitement. 'I'm not much use indoors, but there's something I could try in the garden, if you can get Colin to look out of the window ...' He tails off.

'Well, that might be hard to achieve, my Darlink,' says Dr Krapotkin, not wanting to discourage him. 'But there's no harm in trying, and you never know ...'

'Yes! Yes!' Dug nods furiously.

'Now that just leaves YOU,' says Dr Krapotkin with a tut, turning her attention to Trevor. 'I think it would be fair to say you didn't exactly cover yourself in glory on the last mission did you, Rover?'

'Err, no,' mutters Trevor apologetically.

'Well, here's your chance for redemption, darlink. See that portrait of dear old Doris ...?'

We all look over at the picture the burly mans dumped yesterday. Doris's old mans face stares back. I have to say she does look very kind and friendly.

'I want you to drag it back up to Colin's flat. Not only will he think she's back ... she will be back. And, you can also give me a lift up there too. I'm not missing the action this time. Think you can manage being a pack-horse, Rover? Do a better job than being a doorbell?'

'Trevor no let you down this time,' he woofs. 'Promise.'

'Good, darlink. So that's it. Let's do this thing. Let's send the hideous mans screaming from the block. Let's frighten him to within an inch of his life. Let us terrify, petrify and horrify him. **Let us drive him and his murderous dog from this building FOR EVER!'**

MUMMY RETURNS

When midnight falls, we walk in silence towards the crumbling hidden highway to Flat 5.

I think back to Grandma ignoring my pleas to find a way to save our home. And now here I am, along with my classmates, off to do something ourselves. I feel a strange mix of pride and fear. The elders declared Colin too dangerous to tackle; to succeed, we are going to have to prove them wrong. And if we don't, if he sees us, or if the Duchess catches us ... My mouth suddenly turns as dry as a ball of dust.

We can do this, I tell myself, **we have to do this!** Not just to save our homes, but our lives, and the lives of other pests too.

Dug disappears off towards the garden with a determined look upon his face. He seems very excited about whatever it is he is about to do. Dr Krapotkin, with the help of an upturned plastic container, clambers up on to Trevor's back. 'Giddy up, Rover,' she cries pointing him in the direction of Doris's portrait.

Underlay has worked extremely fast. She struggles over, carrying what looks like the shredded remains of a yellow cardigan, wrapped up in a bit of old skirt. Webbo and I give her a hand carrying it into the tunnel, each of us helping to push the bundle along in front of us. It smells strongly of flowers and biscuits — Doris smelt like a nice person.

Finally, after another long and difficult climb, we reach the air vent. The plan is to wait until we are sure Colin and the Duchess have gone to bed. From the living room we hear the drone of the television. Colin is watching a programme all about a creature called a 'shark', which he and the Duchess seem to be enjoying very much.

'There are sharks in the sewer,' whispers Maximus. 'I beat one up the other day.'

The Plagues laugh so
hard one of them falls out
of his fur.

At last the programme
ends and we hear the pad,
pad of footsteps as Colin
and the Duchess head off
to the bedroom. We wait for the click of the bedroom
light switching off and then we quietly tiptoe out. I feel a
sudden draft of cold air and look up to see Batz swoop
through the now wide-open again window. From the other
end of the hallway comes a faint scraping sound, and
then the click of the front door being quietly opened.

'Still a dab wing at lock-picking,' I hear Dr Krapotkin
cackle to herself. 'Now pop the painting in the living room,
then scarper,' she whispers to Trevor. 'The last thing we
need is you getting spotted, Rover.'

'And you, darlinks,' she says, flapping awkwardly
towards us. 'Underlay, I want you to begin scattering the
clumps of Doris's cardigan around the living room. Batz,
after you've located the thermostat, you head to the

kitchen to help Stix. Start scouting for objects to have some fun with. And Maximus, the fuse box is at the end of the hallway, just outside the kitchen. Get busy, darlink.'

She tells Webbo to wait outside the bedroom door until he is given the signal to get tickling. He heads off looking both petrified and determined.

Everyone disappears and I'm left standing alone in the hallway. I would take a deep breath to steady my nerves, but the stench of bleach is too strong. Instead, I give my body a good shake and then quickly and quietly make my way to the kitchen. Just outside the kitchen door, I pass Maximus using a fat electrical cable to haul himself up the wall, to what must be the fuse box.

I enter the kitchen and wait for Batz to help me get up on the countertop.

'Hey.' She nods coolly as she flies in.

'Hey.' I nod back, trying to sound equally casual.

'So, you need a hand getting up there?'

'Uh-huh,' I say with a shrug.

Using a combination of me scrabbling and her lifting, I finally make it to the top. A huge, white, polished expanse stretches out before me.

'How about you take the coffee maker and the kettle, and I'll take the microwave and the radio?' she puffs.

As I carefully make my way over to the coffee maker, I watch Batz flitting back and forth between the microwave on one side of the room and the radio on the other, checking out how they work and how to turn them on. She is impressively fast. Which I would tell her ... if we were talking. I really miss her and her funny ways.

The coffee maker is a very strange-looking thing: tall and black with a large glass jug on its front. I quickly locate the power switch. The kettle is a further ten mouse bounds along the countertop. It has a long switch that sticks out at the side – I figure jumping on it should do the trick.

'OK, darlinks, I'm about to give Webbo the order to tickle. Prepare yourselves for the big show,' Dr Krapotkin whispers loudly from the hallway.

I feel my stomach lurch. Mice can't actually be sick, but right now I really feel like I could. I clench and unclench my paws, trying to calm myself.

Batz and I wait in silence for what seems like an eternity. But then, finally, we hear it – a panicked cry from the bedroom.

'What the ...? Who was that? Who touched me?'

I imagine Webbo's long, incredibly hairy legs doing terribly tickly things.

'Get off, get off!'

I hear the thud of feet hitting a hard wooden floor.

'Urgh, why's it so cold? What's going on?'

With a loud slam the bedroom door is flung open.

'Put me down! Put me down!' I hear the Duchess yap.

'No, no, my little munchkin, it m-might not be safe,' stammers Colin. The

pad, pad of feet head in our direction. I hear the thwack
of his hand hitting a light switch. For a moment the lights
in the kitchen come on, but then flicker off, then on, then
off again.

'W-w-what's happening?' cries Colin.

He steps into the kitchen and I leap on to the kettle's
switch. With a soft click it turns on and a few moments
later it starts to emit a loud rasping sound. As
I dart across the countertop towards
the coffee machine, I catch a glimpse
of Colin. He's standing frozen
with fear, the Duchess grasped
tightly to his chest.

With a loud whirr the
microwave springs to life.

'I d-don't understand
how—'

With all my might
I press the coffee
machine's switch. It makes
a curious whining noise,

and then begins to bubble like the kettle.

'LET ME DOWN! LET ME DOWN!' protests the Duchess furiously, writhing in his arms.

But Colin isn't listening; he just squeezes her tighter. The lights flash on momentarily, highlighting his face. It's no longer orange but ashen white.

'Oh my gosh, it is her isn't it! Mummy's come back!' he gasps. 'I can smell her! Biscuits and flowers ... she's really here!'

From the corner of the room, an exceptionally happy tune blares from the radio: 'Doo-wap-dee-doo-wap-dee-bap-bang-boo ...'

'Stop it, Mummy, please stop it,' he pleads, looking from one whirring, boiling, bubbling appliance to another. I take this as my chance to get out of the kitchen. I skid to the edge of the countertop and leap.

'Mouse!' yaps the Duchess. 'Mouse! Mouse! Mouse!'

I hit the floor and glance up – has Colin seen me too? Does he understand what she's saying? But clearly Colin doesn't understand, or is too scared to listen.

'You think it's Mummy too, don't you, Duchy-poo?' He

stumbles around, trying to turn everything off. Quick as a flash I skitter across the floor.

'No! I said "Mouse", you numbskull,' the Duchess protests.

I reach the hallway. Above me I hear the fizzing sounds of electric cables and look up to see Maximus crouching inside the open fuse box. He looks extremely pleased with himself. 'Woo-yeah, I'm the master of electric-kery!' he says. 'You may be able to turn a kettle on. But me, I'm the real star ... I can turn stuff OFF ... permanently! Let the master show you how it's done ...' He grabs a length of electric cable between his front paws and opens his huge mouth wide ...

'No, Maximus! Dr Krapotkin said don—!' But it's too late. His huge teeth slam together like a pair of vicious scissors.

KERBANG!

I'm blinded by a sudden flash of intense bright light, then everything goes dark. Next to me, I hear a loud **THUD** and the acrid smell of burning hair suddenly fills my nose. I look down and see Maximus has been flung from the fuse box and is now lying lifeless next to me.

'Wake up, you fat lump of fur, wake up!' shouts Plague One, pummelling his chest.

'Oh, what a night, Oh, I got a funny feeeeeling ...' sings a happy voice. The radio is still on: it must be battery-powered.

'Please, Maximus, please!' I hear Plague Two cry. 'Can't you feel us biting you?'

But Maximus isn't moving. He's badly injured, maybe worse. I should try and help save him. But isn't this what I said I wanted? Maximus to be gone for ever? Here's my chance to never see him again, never hear him say another horrible word or do another nasty thing.

I hear Colin fumbling around in the dark, trying to turn off the radio. I've got to make a decision, fast. No one else has seen him, I'm the only one who can help. But it's also my opportunity to escape ...

The radio goes silent.

'I smell rat!' I hear the Duchess yap. 'Let me at it, let me at it!'

I can't leave him. Something deep inside won't let me. He may be horrible, but I'm not. I try desperately to remember the rules of ... what was it? CPD? CPT? I can't even recall its silly name.

'I'll rip out its heart and dine on its lungs,' I hear the Duchess snarl.

That's it ... lungs! I need to check and see if he's breathing. I press my ear close to his enormous nose. I hear nothing.

'You got to do that blow-in-the-mouth thing, dude!' says Webbo, scuttling over.

I look at Maximus's hairy mouth, at his enormous teeth.

Surely I can't.

But I have to ...

With a shudder, I reach forward, clamp his nose closed with one paw and pull his mouth open with the other. I am not sure which smells worst: his burnt fur or foul breath.

'Do it! Do it!' beg the Plagues. 'Hurry!'

I inhale, place my mouth over his ... and blow.

I look at Maximus's chest. Nothing.

'Puff harder!' cries Plague One. 'His lungs are bigger than yours!'

I take another breath, the biggest I possibly can, and then blow, hard.

Maximus's eyes fly open. He looks straight at me, sees my mouth clamped over his.

'EURGH! EURGH! GET OFF! GET OFF! WHAT ARE YOU DOING KISSING ME?' he cries, leaping to his feet and shoving

me away. I tumble down the hallway, straight into the pathway of the oncoming Colin. The Duchess goes into a crazed fit. With one final writhing twist, she at last frees herself. She drops to the floor in front of me.

'Duchess! My princess, come back!' cries Colin. 'It's not safe ...'

She stares down at me, her beady black eyes glistening with excitement.

And for the second time in as many days, I hear Grandma's words in my ears.

Look a dog in the eye, seconds later you will die ...

This is what she meant. And this time, there's no escape.

BATTLE ROY-ALE

'So, bottom-biter,' the Duchess sneers, licking her lips. 'It's payback time.'

'Run, Stix, run!' shouts Webbo, scrambling up the wall out of her reach.

His words snap me into action, and I turn

and sprint as fast as I can.

'Will you please stop this running away business,' snarls the Duchess, bounding after me. She's so close I can feel her breath on my back. I race into the living room and shoot up the side of one of the boxes.

The Duchess rears up, landing her paws on the edge of it.

'Got you now, mouse,' she snarls, snapping at me. I leap backwards. Beneath my feet, I glimpse the words, 'Ultra Fast Mouse Poison'. I'm not sure which would be worse, being poisoned or being bitten in half.

'What are you doing, Duchess?' cries Colin, stumbling into the living room behind us.

Surely he's going to see me now. But, just as he approaches, I hear the click of a torch being switched on and in the corner of the room the portrait of Doris is suddenly illuminated.

Clever Trevor didn't let us down this time. As I look at it, I'm sure I see Doris's left eye blink. Colin spins round just in time to see. His hands fly to his face and he lets out an ear-splitting cry of horror. 'MUMMY!' he cries. 'But how did you ... I mean ... you really are back! And you look so ...'

Doris's left eye narrows.

'... angry.'

I smile to myself. I knew Dr Krapotkin would be up to something clever.

'I can't take this torment any more,' stammers a terrified Colin. 'We're going! We're leaving right now! Come on, Duchess ...'

'How can you be so gullible, you fool?' yaps the Duchess, swiping at Colin with her claws as he tries to pick her up. He reels back in horror. **'It's not Doris, it's filthy PESTS!'**

With all her might the Duchess shoves the box. It topples over taking me with it ...

'Stix, over here!' I hear Batz shout.

Out of the corner of my eye, I glimpse her banging on the window, trying to get my attention. It's going to take a mighty leap to reach it, but it's that or land on the floor where the Duchess can easily get me. I fling myself from the tumbling box up into the air ...

I make it — just — skidding across the ledge and slamming into the glass.

The Duchess turns towards me and smiles evilly. She realises what I have just done — **that I'm backed against the window, with no escape**. What was Batz thinking?!

'Stix, dude, no!' I hear Webbo cry. I look across and see him tucked into a fold of the curtain. 'Hey, nasty dog, get me! Come on! It was my turn, remember?' He calls out to the Duchess and scuttles away, up towards the curtain rail, trying to get her to chase him instead.

'No chance,' the Duchess snarls. 'The rodent has much more meat on its bones.'

'Come on!' begs Colin, stumbling towards us in the darkness. 'Duchess, what are you doing? We need to get out of here!'

The Duchess doesn't answer. Instead, she prowls towards me. I feel the cold glass of the window press against my back and begin to shake with fear. I'm trapped.

I hear Colin trip over the upturned box. He tumbles to his knees.

'Has she put a spell on you, baby?' I hear him snivel as he crawls towards her. 'Please, please, come on.'

I cast my eyes around the room, looking for an escape. I can see Dr Krapotkin looking out from behind the painting, her eyes wide with fear. Tucked away under the sofa I spot the cowering shape of Maximus. Typical that I save him, only for him to do nothing to try and rescue me.

But it's too late anyway. 'Here I come ... ready or not,' growls the Duchess, drawing her body back, readying to pounce.

And that's when I hear Batz at the window. 'Don't worry,' she mouths.

DON'T WORRY? Is she MAD?!

The Duchess launches herself at me. She leaps up, her body gliding through the air like a flying mop.

This is it, there's no way out.

Her enormous mouth fills my entire vision.

I close my eyes.

My fate is sealed.

This is what it feels like to be swallowed ...

... whole.

Then, just as her jaws are about to slam closed, I feel a sudden gust of cold air from behind me.

IT ALL GOES OUT OF THE WINDOW

I'm falling.

Not into the Duchess's mouth but ...

... backwards ...

... out of the window.

My eyes fly open. How did the window suddenly open? The Duchess looks equally surprised as she sails out of the window behind me.

As I topple out into the darkness, I look up and see Batz. She's the one who opened it. She's grinning. WHAT? NO WAY! Did she mean for me to fall out? Did she want this to happen?

'HELP! HELP!' cries the Duchess, frantically paddling her legs in mid-air, like somehow they are going to help her fly. But they're not, and we're both falling, falling, plummeting through the darkness towards the garden below.

I close my eyes tight, readying myself for the short, sharp pain of inevitable death. But instead, I feel the stab of claws in my back and hear the frantic flap of wings. I look up and see Batz above me, her face twisted with the strain of holding me up. 'Geeez, first I lift you on to the countertop, and now this ...' she groans, through tightly gritted teeth.

Up, up she lifts me, her wings beating hard against her body. We're right back up by the window now. 'If I can just get you to the gutter ...' she says and, a moment later, we're tumbling into the leaf-filled gutter at the top of the building.

We hear a loud scream from below. '**AHHHH!!!!!**' wails Colin, '**AHHHHHHHHHHHHHHHHHHH!**'

We peek over the lip of the gutter and see what he has seen. There, written in huge letters across the garden, in freshly dug soil, are the words:

GET OWT BAD COLIN!

And in the middle of the O of OWT, lies the Duchess's motionless body.

'Mummy, no! You've taken my darling Duchess,' sobs Colin. 'Oh, I can't even bear to look at her ... my poor heart can't take it. Surely now you've punished me enough. Please, please just let me leave in peace.'

Batz and I fall back happily into the leaves. My heart pounds like a Maximus-sized fist in my chest. I can't believe we actually did it – we've got rid of the Duchess.

'OMG! OMG!' says Batz, her eyes wide with surprise. 'I think I just, err ... killed a dog.'

'Well, she was the one that jumped out of the window,' I reply. 'So, technically, it was kind of her fault.'

'Heehahahahaha, good point!' she laughs. 'And talking of jumping out of the window, you should have seen your face! Did you really think I was going to let you plummet to your death?'

'I mean ... err ... I did wonder ... we've not really been getting on ...'

'Well, you did call me a big-mouthed, stupid bat.' She frowns.

'I know, I know, that wasn't nice. It's just I was hurt because you didn't seem bothered about leaving. And, and you didn't even want to hang out any more,' I reply, a knot of embarrassment twisting inside me.

'What? When?' she says indignantly.

'You know, the other night. I said, "Hide and seek?" and you said you had to go and see a gnat or something.'

'Jeez, no, no! I had to go home ... I'd been grounded.'

'Grounded ... but why didn't you just say so?'

'Because ... I, err ... gave my brother a black eye for teasing me about being best friends with a mouse. Sorry, you're right. I should have said – it's just ... I didn't want you to think my family has a thing against mice. I never meant to upset you.'

'I'm sorry too,' I say, suddenly feeling rather ashamed of how angry I got with her. 'I shouldn't have jumped to conclusions. I just got it into my head that you didn't want to be my friend and that's all I could think about.'

'Well ... I don't just want to be your friend.' She smiles at me. 'I want to be your **best** friend.' And with that she throws her wings around me and gives me the biggest hug ever.

'Now, come on,' she says. 'Let's go and meet the others in the basement. Bet they'll be wondering what happened to you!'

THE D-WORD

By the time Batz and I get back to the basement, everyone
is gathering back in the wardrobe.

'**Hoorah! Stix lives**,' cries Webbo as I bound off the end
of the lampshade.

'All thanks to Batz,' I say, giving her a little wink.

'Oh, Darlinks, I am so pleased you are both back in one
piece,' says Dr Krapotkin clasping her good wing to her
chest.

I notice Underlay has replaced the shred of carpet
she always carries with a small ball of Doris's cardigan.
'Iwantedamementoofthegreatbattle,' she grins.

Maximus is slumped in his usual seat in the back. He

looks terrible. He's missing a patch of fur on one side of his body and has a large bump on the side of his head. I glance over at him, he meets my eyes for a moment and then looks away. Clearly saving his life hasn't made him like me any more.

Everyone is back except Dug. I guess he's tired – he did A LOT of digging.

'What a fantastic job you have all done,' continues Dr Krapotkin wiping a tear from her eye. 'You've made this old pigeon prouder that she can ever express. Colin is packing his bag as we speak, and the dog is gone, gone, gone. It is the triumph of all triumphs. Well done, everyone!'

'Hey, mouse ... we did good, we did good,' woofs Trevor excitedly, taking a seat next to me. His tail starts to wag so madly it nearly knocks me over. 'Ooops. Sorry!' he says. 'I just so pleased.'

'Me too,' I reply.

'And me three!' cries Batz with a laugh, swooping down and sitting next to us.

'Now, there is just one small thing we need to talk about,' says Dr Krapotkin, her voice dropping to a whisper.

'You must NEVER be telling your elders about this, darlinks. Not a single word about what we did. I would most definitely lose my job for gross misconduct – one thousand and ten per cent.'

What? No way! We just had undoubtedly **the most epic battle of our lives** in which we stopped not only the Duchess eating us all, but also stopped Colin turning the block into an Emporium of Pesticides, and we are not going to be able to breathe a word about it? I can't believe I'm not going to be able to tell Grandma we proved her and the elders wrong.

'Now, let us all celebrate, my darlinks,' she coos pulling two mouldy hunks of bread out from underneath her wing, 'with a fine, vintage slice of white.'

The bread might be covered in hairy green mould, but I don't care – I'm starving.

'Ahh,' says Dr Krapotkin, between pecks at the crust. 'The sweet, sweet taste of victory.'

'Soon to be the bitter tang of defeat!' snarls a voice from across the basement.

My heart plummets.

The chunk of bread I'm eating slips from my grasp.

Because there, at the top of the basement stairs stands ...

... the Duchess!

She's filthy. Her once shiny coat is now matted with mud and tufts of grass. The bow in her hair hangs, grimy and tattered.

But her nasty little eyes are still bright, and she seems to have lost none of her vileness.

'I found THIS in the garden,' she says, pushing a round, furry lump forwards with her paw. 'I believe it might be yours.'

'S-sorry guys,' whimpers Dug, struggling to his feet. 'I thought she was dea—'

'Shut up!' she snaps, shoving him back down. 'Now, you may think your little plan has worked. But I'm going to show my ignoramus halfwit owner that it wasn't the ghost of his batty mother that came to give him a sign, but YOU, you repellent bunch of filth-bags. Now, here's the deal. You're going to give yourselves up, show it was you all along, or Moley here is going to be, how shall we say ... an ex-Moley. And we wouldn't want that now, would we? I mean, just look at his cute little face ...' She turns Dug's head round to face us – he looks petrified. 'Who would want to see this poor little fur-ball get hurt?' she says, drawing a long, sharp claw down his tear-stained cheek.

'Your plan has a big hole in it,' says Dr Krapotkin. 'The mans is leaving right now. You're going to have to suck it up, darlink. We "filth-bags" won.'

'I shan't be sucking anything up, DARLINK,' smirks the Duchess, shoving Dug down the last few steps and dragging him to the centre of the room. 'Colin may be packing, but on his way out he will be paying a little visit to this hellhole, where he will find you sitting in the middle of this manky old rug, all cooing and howling, showing off all the tricks of your stupid hoax!'

'Why would that disgusting mans dare to come down here after the scare we gave him?' Dr Krapotkin laughs.

'Why? Ha! Because of this, you manky old pigeon!' The Duchess points to a large button on her sparkly collar. 'This is what you call a "FindMyDoggy" collar. When I press this button, Colin will see an alert on his phone, know I am alive, know EXACTLY where I am, and come running. So clever!'

'ARGHHH, technology be damned,' Dr Krapotkin mutters under her breath.

'Now, if you wouldn't mind all coming over

here and arranging yourselves neatly on the rug,' the Duchess says, 'we can have this little misunderstanding sorted out in no time at all. Oh, and I should point out, just to be fair, that I can't guarantee what Colin will do with you all. Perhaps you can be the first victims of his testing laboratory or maybe, hopefully, he will let me share the slaughter. Oh, and you – you flea-infested lump of sausage dog – I'll see he sends you off to the doggy rescue centre.'

'I told you, I got no fleas,' snarls Trevor. 'I got collar.'

'Flea collars are for ugly mongrels that no one will want to adopt.' She laughs. 'No doubt it will be a brief stay at the centre, followed by a swift visit to the vet for a special "goodnight injection".'

'Not the vet,' whimpers Trevor, shuffling across to the rug with his tail between his legs. 'Trevor scared of vet.'

'Now,' says the Duchess, slamming Dug down on the rug and pinning him there with a hairy paw, 'do come and join us, won't you?'

Reluctantly, we all make our way over. We have no choice – we can't let her hurt him. Trevor takes a seat on one side of me and Batz on the other. I catch her eye; she looks as scared as I feel. How has this all gone so wrong so fast?

'Good,' says the Duchess as, with a big grin on her face, she presses the button on her collar.

FARTS 'N' FLEAS

A little blue light in the centre of the Duchess's collar starts to flash.

I hope and pray that Colin has already left, or at least that his phone has run out of charge.

Please don't come down and find us, I pray. **Please ...** I cross all my fingers and my toes so hard it hurts.

'Any minute now ...' says the Duchess gleefully.

And then we hear them, the dreaded thud of mans footsteps. 'Duchess?' comes Colin's surprised cry from the hallway above. 'Duchess, my darling, where are you? I thought you were d-dead ...'

Trevor's tummy gives a loud rumble, and then another. I look over at him. He looks back nervously, shifting uncomfortably.

'Sit still,' snaps the Duchess.

But Trevor can't. His tummy grumbles again, this time even louder. Then ...

PRRRRRRRRARRRRRRRPPPPPPPPPPPP!

'Sorry,' he mutters, 'mouldy bread do bad things to Trevor's tummy!'

'What the ...' gasps the Duchess. 'That's disgust—' She coughs, her whole body heaving and retching violently. Then, finally, with one mighty heave she coughs up a large lump of black goo.

'You fowl, repellent creature.' She snarls, recomposing herself. 'I'm going to make Moley here pay for that hideous, odious ...'

But just as she begins to press down on poor Dug's already quite flattened body, we hear the creak of the basement door.

'Here, here, over here!' yaps the Duchess, as the basement door creaks open. 'Look, here's the disgusting mole that dug up your lawn ...'

'Duchy-Wutchy! Is that really you? Did Mummy not actually do you in?' calls Colin, stumbling down the stairs, a large suitcase clattering behind him. 'I'm coming, I'm coming ...'

'And these are the horrible pests that have been tricking you too!' she yaps excitedly, pressing down yet harder on poor Dug. His tiny eyes bulge in his head.

I try to catch Batz's eye – we can't let this happen. We can't let everything we have just done count for nothing. Colin can't know it was us and not Doris. 'We've got to do something,' I whisper.

We're both desperately looking around the basement for something that can help us, and that's when my eyes settle on the big bag of cement.

Batz follows my gaze – she sees it too.

'Ghost dog?' she whispers, and motions pushing the bag off the shelf with her wings. **Yes**, I nod, knowing exactly what it is I need to do.

'Hey Duchy-Wuchy!' I call, trying desperately to hide the tremor in my voice. 'Come on, let's finish our battle once and for all.'

She stares down at me, her eyes narrowing to slits.

'Come on, you and me,' I say. 'That's what you want, isn't it?'

A slight grin plays across her lips. But she doesn't move.

'Surely you're not scared of a mouse?' I taunt. 'A teeny-tiny mouse?'

'Of course I'm not,' she sneers, taking a small step forwards. Dug seizes his chance and wiggles free from her grasp, but the Duchess doesn't notice, her eyes have glazed over, all her attention is on now 1000 per cent on me. 'I'll rip your little head off.' She snarls.

'Oh, you think you will?' I say, taking a step backwards. 'Clearly you've never met a ninja mouse before! See these paws? Fast as lightning, sharp as swords!' I can't believe I'm saying this stuff. But it seems to be working. The Duchess takes another step forwards, and then another.

'What are you doing, darlink?' screeches Dr Krapotkin, 'Are you crazy? There's still time to run and hide.'

But I keep going. I'm slowly edging back and back, till I'm nearly under the shelf. The Duchess stalks after me, a thin line of drool dripping from her mouth.

'I'm going to slice and dice and tear your body limb from limb,' she says, readying to pounce. 'There's no mouse in the world who can beat me.'

I take one last step back.

As she leaps forward, I neatly jump to the side and BOOMPH! the bag of cement powder engulfs us both. I can't see a thing.

'**ATCHOO! ATCHOO!**' she sneezes.

'Duchy-poo?' calls Colin, hauling his suitcase through the piles of junk and boxes.

I've got to move – get away before he reaches us. But

I can't. **My tail is trapped.** I struggle to pull it free, but it won't budge. As the cloud of powder clears I see, to my horror ...

'Gotcha!' beams the Duchess, pressing her paw down harder on my tail. She's completely white, from head to

toe. And so, I realise, am I.

'Say goodbye to the world, mouse!' she shrieks, licking her lips. 'Take your last breath before I bite off your stupid head.'

No! No! No! How can this be happening again!

I try desperately to yank my tail from her grasp.

But I can't.

Her mouth opens.

Please make it painless, I beg, squeezing my eyes closed.

But then ...

'Oi, you, you mangy old fleabag, get your paws off the mouse!'

It's Maximus, and he's bounding towards us.

'What?' says the Duchess, her head snapping round. 'What did you just say?'

'I said, let go of the mouse ... you mangy old fleabag.' He pulls himself up to his full height. I can't believe it. Surely he can't really be trying to help me?

'Fleas? How dare you! I don't have fleas!' snarls the Duchess indignantly.

'You do now ...' replies Maximus with a grin. 'Plagues – infest!'

'Hurray! Pedigree blood!' they both cheer, as the two of them leap from his coat into hers. 'Our pleasure!'

'Argh-urgh!!!' the Duchess

cries, falling to the floor. Her body starts to twitch as the Plagues go into a biting frenzy. 'Ouch ... ouch ... get off! GET OFF!'

Maximus and I dive behind a pile of old magazines as, just at that moment, Colin finally reaches the Duchess. He stares down at her, his eyes widening in horror at the twitching, jerking, terrifying ....

'**AHHHHHHHHHHHHHHHHHHHHH!**' he cries, letting out a scream so loud and high it forces me to cover my ears. 'GHOST! YOU'RE A GHOST, TOO! Oh, my Duchess ... I knew you were dead, I never should have come, I'm sorry, I'm so sorry!' he gabbles, as he turns and stumbles back towards the stairs.

'No wait!' yaps the Duchess, desperately trying to chase after him.

'Get away! Get away!' he shouts, shooing her flinching body back with his foot.

He reaches the stairs. His suitcase clatters on every step as he frantically hauls it up as fast as he can.

'It's j-just ... ouch – argh – argggggghh – f-fleas!' the Duchess howls, dragging herself up the steps behind him. 'P-please wait!'

'Leave me alone!' cries Colin, kicking at her with his foot. 'Just leave me alone! I don't want to be haunted by a dog as well.' He disappears through the door, the shuddering and twitching Duchess following after him.

'Ha! Ha! Ha!' laughs Trevor. 'Bet you wish you have flea collar now!'

BIG, HAIRY, RATS

This time we've done it. No doubt about it. The Plagues return telling us they watched Colin drive away, leaving the Duchess howling on the pavement, where she was picked up soon after by the Dog Rescue Service, who concluded from her injuries and the state she was in that not only had she been abandoned but also mistreated.

'Well done, Stix and Batz, that was terrific!' says Dr Krapotkin, clapping her wings. 'You had me worried there a moment, but amazing, darlinks – a true stroke of brilliance.'

'And Maximus helped too,' I say, looking around at him, surprised he's not bigging himself up as usual. 'She'd have bitten my head off if it wasn't for you.'

'Well, I kind of owed you,' he mutters grudgingly.

'Yes! Yes! Thank you also, Maximus, darlink, for your quick thinking. Are you OK, darlink?' she asks. 'You seem awfully quiet.'

'He's still in shock from actually beating a dog,' laughs Plague One.

'Though it was us that did all the hard work,' sniggers Plague Two.

'SHUT UP!' snarls Maximus, swatting at his left ear.

From behind us Dug let's out a shocked cry. 'Look!' he says pointing at the gooey lump of sick the Duchess coughed up. 'It's moving.'

We all gather around, the disgusting lump is indeed wiggling. One shiny, black leg shoots out, and then another. It can't be ... surely it's not ...

'Blue!' cries Dug pulling at the goo with his large paws.

'Yezzz, itzzzz me,' coughs Blue struggling free of the gloopy mess. 'Dogzzz zzztomachs are one crazzzy place.'

He's back. Our class is complete again. We all gather around clapping and cheering.

'Well, this truly is an extraordinarily amazing and happy moment.' Dr Krapotkin claps her wings together. 'Now we can really celebrate!' She pauses to look at us all with a smile and I'm sure I can see a tear in her eye. 'I think it is now most definitely time I send word for the elders to return. And remember, none of this ever happened, OK?' she says, tapping her beak.

'We'd better get all this powder off you then, Stix. Don't want to leave any clues.' Dug gently dusts me from head to toe with his large paws.

'Ibetitwasreallydarkandsmelly,' Underlay says to Blue with a shudder.

'Not as smelly as Trev's epic fart!' giggles Webbo. 'That was off the chart, dude!'

'You're welcome,' he says, smiling proudly. 'And now

Trevor have to go home. Owners probably wondering where he gone.'

It doesn't take long for all the elders to start arriving. It is so good to see Grandma. 'My boy! What's been going on?' she says, wrapping her arms around me. 'What's this I hear about that horrible mans leaving?'

Luckily, before I'm forced to lie, Dr Krapotkin clears her throat and announces that, due to 'unexpected and unexplained circumstances', Colin and the Duchess have left and will never be returning. **'Ever again!'** she finishes forcefully.

Dug's pa cocks his head to one side, eyeing her suspiciously. 'Well, that certainly is a turn-up for the books. And you had nothing to do with this, Lyudmila?' he asks sceptically.

'Absolutely not, darlink,' she coos innocently. 'Nothing at all.'

Everyone is pleased and very relieved. I overhear Batz's parents telling her that they had found a church roof to live in but were worried the bell would keep them awake. Blue's parents were about to move into a bin van, but were concerned about getting accidently mashed in the crusher. And Dug's family had found a golf course to live on but were worried about being constantly hit on the head by falling balls. All in all, everyone's glad that they get to stay.

Maximus's parents are the last to arrive. They barge through everyone, knocking them out of their way. They are so HUGE they dwarf Maximus. 'What's all this?' snarls his pa. 'What are you all doing back?'

Dr Krapotkin calmly explains, for the second time, how Colin has gone.

'So now there'll be no posh stuff coming down the pipes?' spits his ma. 'No upgrade to our diet?'

'H-he wasn't b-building new flats,' stammers Maximus nervously. I've never seen him look so afraid. Even the Duchess didn't scare him this much.

'WHAT DID YOU JUST SAY?' snaps his ma, grabbing him by his ear and lifting him up off the ground.

'Did you just answer me back, you pathetic little pip-squeak?'

'I w-wasn't. I was j-just s-saying ...' stammers Maximus, wincing in pain.

'Did you have something to do with them leaving?' she growls, pulling him up to her eye level, twisting his ear yet further. 'Did you and your pathetic classmates **DO** something?' For a moment I think he's going to tell them everything.

'No!' he says defiantly. 'We didn't do anything.'

'Good,' she snarls, letting go of his ear. 'I'd have hated to have to really punish you.'

Maximus falls to the floor, clutching the side of his head. **Poor Maximus.** I know just how that feels.

He frantically rubs a tear from his eye, trying not to show the pain he's in.

'The Raticuses,' whispers Grandma, putting her arm around me. 'A truly despicable bunch.'

Before all this, I would have agreed. But I suddenly feel sorry for Maximus. It must be terrible to grow up with such cruel and nasty parents.

As crazy as it sounds, maybe I should give him a chance. After all, he did save my life; maybe, one day, we might actually be friends.

I catch his eye and smile sympathetically.

'What you looking at, mini mouse?' he sneers.

OK, I guess maybe we won't.

BACK TO THE BOTTOM

Grandma and I say our goodbyes to everyone and head off home. We find the kitchen just as we left it, piled high with boxes. And the washing machine, with our nest tucked away behind it, still right where it was, next to the kitchen cabinets.

The clock on the oven says 7.05. The mans will be up any minute. I check Trevor's bed, but he's not there. Then, from the hallway, I hear a faint whining and a scratching of paws on wood.

'That's odd – what's Trevor doing out there?' says Grandma.

I hear the pad of MyLove's feet, followed by the creak of The Frontier Door opening.

'Trevor!' he cries. 'There you are, boy! Schnookums come quick – Trevor's back! We've been so worried about you. Where have you been?'

Oh, no! I suddenly panic. What if Trevor says something, gives the game away? The mans won't understand, of course, but Grandma will.

'Was just looking for an old bone in the garden,' he woofs, brushing past them and slumping down exhaustedly in his bed.

I breathe a quiet sigh of relief.

'And what's this?' I hear Schnookums say. 'There's a note on the doormat. It's ... it's from Colin ... looks like it's been scribbled in a terrible hurry ... It just says ... "Sorry, all tenants can stay, rent remains same, best wishes, Colin Royale." I can't believe it!'

'Oh, my gosh!' cries MyLove. 'Really? That's the best news ever! I wonder what on earth made him change his mind?'

'Me too,' says Grandma, eyeing me suspiciously. 'Are you sure you don't have any idea why Colin left in such a hurry?'

'Come on,' I laugh, 'what could we young 'uns have possibly done to such a dangerous mans? You said yourself he was unbeatable.'

'Well, yes, it would have taken an extremely clever and courageous act to drive him away,' she says with a smile. 'I mean, one so enormous in magnitude that those involved would be heralded as heroes for life ... if, of course, they ever admitted to what they had done ...'

I'm dying to tell her. The truth literally feels like fire in my stomach, burning to escape. **But a promise is a promise.**

So instead I smile back and with a casual shrug say, 'Yeah, but really, what kind of a fool wouldn't own up to doing something that great?'

The mans spend the rest of the day unpacking while Grandma and I both sleep. By the time we rise, the place is back to just the way it was, right down to the tasty, sticky mess underneath Boo-Boo's chair – leftover strawberry jam on toast! Another favourite of mine.

Grandma goes back to bed not long after we've finished and, like usual, I find myself alone in the kitchen with Trevor, who is lying on his bed, fast asleep.

Now I'm back home and everything is back to the way it was, it's hard to believe any of our crazy adventure ever happened.

Perhaps now would be a good time to try another somersault over his bottom? After the epic fart in the basement, I should be safe this time.

I walk to the far corner of the kitchen. I'm just drawing the last of my lucky four breaths, when BOOMPF! Something slams into me, knocking me off my feet.

'**Heehahahaha!** Didn't see that one coming, did you?' squeals Batz, pressing her big face up against mine.

'You really are a massive pain in the behind,' I say, pulling myself to my feet, though secretly I'm very pleased to see her.

'Yeah, but I'm YOUR pain in the behind.' She smiles. 'Allllllll yours! So, what we doing? Are you jumping over Trev's bottom again? Need a hand? You jump, I'll lift you? I've had quite a bit of practice recently.'

'**Hey, leave my bottom alone!**' comes a sulky woof from across the kitchen. I look over and see Trevor watching us. Surely he can't have gone back to being grumpy so quickly?

'Aw, now come on, Trev, don't be such a spoilsport,' says Batz teasingly. 'I mean, it's only one little jump – what's that between friends?'

'Oh, OK, go on then,' he replies, rolling his eyes. 'I suppose as it's you two.'

'Come on, Stix, you ready for the big one?' Batz grins.

I look up at her hovering above me, her eyes wide with excitement.

'OK,' I say, taking one last deep breath. **'Let's do it!'**

Seriously, Stix and Batz, stop drawing on my face!

Emer started her career working in the advertising industry, where she helped create the famous John Lewis Christmas ads. But, after her first series of books, **The Diaries of Pig**, became a bestseller, she quit advertising to become a full-time author. Always looking for ideas in the world around her, Emer alighted on the idea for **PESTS** after she was woken early one morning by an extremely loud pigeon cooing outside her bedroom window. As she lay angrily in bed, cursing the bird for waking her, a thought sprang to her mind – what if there was a school where creatures were taught how to do such pesty, annoying things? **Return Of The Pests** is the second in this mad-cap series and she hopes you enjoy reading it as much as she enjoyed writing it.

If you'd like to see more of Stix and the PESTS gang,
you can find them here . . .
PESTS website: www.pestsbook.com
Emer's website: www.emerstamp.com
Emer's YouTube channel: The World of Emer Stamp
(Pssst... Did you find the hidden message on the edge of the
book? Check out the PESTS website for more secrets, games and
all kinds of pesty fun. But remember, it's for **PESTS ONLY!**)